BEACHSIDE MEMORIES

MARIGOLD ISLAND BOOK FIVE

FIONA BAKER

Copyright © 2021 by Fiona Baker

All rights reserved.

No part of this publication may be reproduced, distributed, or transmitted in any form, including photocopying, recording, or other electronic or mechanical methods, without the prior written permission of the publisher, except in the case of brief quotations for reviews or certain other noncommercial uses.

This is a work of fiction. Any resemblance to actual people, living or dead, or actual events is purely coincidental.

CHAPTER ONE

Grace Nelson breathed a sigh of relief when the tiny plane she had taken from Boston to Marigold Island finally touched down. Even though the weather was lovely, a warm early summer day, she still felt every single bump in the air along the way. It was a necessary evil, though—Marigold's airport was just as small as the plane was, so she wasn't expecting a smooth ride like she would have on a big jet.

The pilot's voice crackled over the speaker. "Welcome to Marigold Island. Hang tight for a bit with your seatbelts fastened, folks."

"Well, there's not much else we can do, is there?" The older woman sitting next to Grace chuckled as she spoke.

"Nope." Grace sighed, restlessness making her

shift in her seat as she looked out the small window. She could see the rich blue waters not too far off in the distance, the heat coming up in waves from the concrete between her and the ocean. It had been a long time since she'd been back to Marigold, but so far, it looked nearly the same as it had when she'd been a teenager.

"What brings you to the island?" the woman beside her asked.

"I'm returning home, more or less. I used to live here when I was growing up. My family—well, my dad and I, since my mom passed when I was young—moved away when I was eighteen," Grace said. "And I went off to college, then started my career as a photographer, so I never really had a reason to come visit until now."

"Did someone in your family move back here?"

"Ah, not really." Grace played with the end of her dark ponytail. "I'm just visiting to see some friends who recently moved back to the island. My father passed away not too long ago, and I need a break to figure out what to do with my life."

"I'm so sorry, honey," the woman said. Something about her expression made the words truly touch Grace's heart.

"Thank you." Grace smiled gently, looking down

at her hands. "I was his full-time caretaker for a long time, since he had early onset dementia. If there's any small silver lining, it's that I was there for him to the end."

"You're a good daughter."

Grace thanked the woman again, a familiar sad ache filling her chest. She was an only child, so it had been just her and her dad ever since she was a little girl. Seeing him slowly slip away mentally and emotionally while still being physically present was one of the hardest things she'd ever had to deal with, but now she hoped he was at peace wherever he was.

She'd brought his ashes with her, since Marigold had always been one of his favorite places. All of the reading she had done on properly grieving had helped to some degree, but she hoped that finding the perfect place to spread his ashes and celebrate his life would fully renew her spirits.

"All right, folks. Feel free to unfasten your seatbelts and head out. Have a great day, and we hope to see you again," the pilot said.

"Take care, okay?" the older woman said to Grace, gently squeezing her hand. "I hope you find what you're looking for and what you need here."

Grace squeezed her hand back. It had been so long since she had connected like this, even on a small level, with a total stranger. Many days, she felt like she just spoke with her father's doctors or nurses, or the local pharmacist. Meeting someone new was a nice change of pace, hopefully the first of many.

Marigold's airport still looked almost the same as it had when she'd moved away nearly twenty years before, with its retro carpeting and small, cramped baggage claim area. It was too small to support big stores or restaurants like Denver's airport did, but that was part of its charm. There was one little souvenir shop and a place to get a cup of coffee before boarding.

She hadn't been old enough to rent a car the last time she'd been in town, so it took a while to figure out where to go. But once she found the rental car place, she got a car, put her bags inside, and drove across the island toward the Beachside Inn. She navigated the streets almost on auto-pilot, to her surprise. The roads were just the same, lined with trees and fragrant plants. Cute, inviting homes appeared from time to time, then more frequently as she got closer to town.

She rolled down the car window as she pulled onto a main road, letting the early June air and the smell of salt toss her dark hair around. A grin spread across her face when she made a turn to go into town. In just a few short minutes, she would finally see her friends after years and years apart.

* * *

It usually didn't take Lydia Walker long to confirm the Beachside Inn's calendar of events, but today was different. She kept pausing to look at the sparkling engagement ring on her left hand instead of just checking off things on her to-do list. She couldn't help herself. Her fiancé—and it felt so nice to be able to call him that—had given her the most perfect ring, along with a perfect proposal.

She smiled to herself and dragged her eyes away from her hand. Every time she looked at the ring, she was struck with how happy she was that she and Grant had found each other, despite the fact that neither of them had even been looking for love after losing people they had cared about. So much of her life had changed, and she was excited to see how the future was going to pan out. She never would have thought she'd feel this way when she'd been lost in the fog of grief after her first husband Paul's death.

"Lydia, is that ring hypnotizing you?" Angela Collins, one of Lydia's best friends and the co-owner of the inn, asked as she walked into the office.

"What?" Lydia looked up and grinned. "No. I swear it's not."

"Uh-huh." Angela grinned back, brushing her honey-blonde hair over her shoulder. "I don't blame you, though. I just came back here to check on you since Kathy's at the front desk."

Their endlessly helpful employee, Kathy, was a pro at the front desk by now. Both of them were completely comfortable letting her have free rein while they worked on other things.

"Things are going a little slowly." Lydia checked the time, which felt like it was crawling by. "I think it's just because I know Grace will be arriving soon, and I can't wait."

"I feel the same way! It's like time is moving at half speed." Angela sighed and sat down at her desk. "I think she's probably landed by now, right?"

"I think so. I'm so excited for her to finally get here. It feels like we've been talking about her coming to visit for ages now, and it's finally the day," Lydia said.

"Yeah, ditto. And we can truly catch up."

"Definitely. As much as I love talking on the phone with her, seeing her face to face is going to be better."

Lydia checked the time again, as if any progress

might have been made in the five seconds since she had checked before. But she was honestly that excited. Reconnecting with Angela had felt so easy, as if no time had passed at all, and it had led to this amazing business and her new life. Lydia couldn't wait to see where Grace's arrival took them all.

The bell on the front door jingled, making both women perk up. They looked at each other with a grin. It had to be Grace.

CHAPTER TWO

Grace looked up at the Beachside Inn, hardly believing her eyes. She was very familiar with the building from the years she had spent living in Marigold as a kid. Back then, it had been one of the most beautiful buildings on the entire island, drawing tourists who weren't even staying there to come look at it. It was difficult to live on the island and *not* hear about it, especially in the summer

It still appeared just as stately and vintage as she remembered, but at the same time, it looked new. Its grayish roof looked like it had been replaced recently, and the white siding had definitely gotten a fresh coat of paint. The big wraparound porch looked just as inviting as it always had, with rocking chairs on either side of the door and beautiful landscaping leading up to it. She wondered if the bay windows still had the comfortable seats that she, Angela, and Lydia had loved to sit on.

When she stepped inside, her jaw dropped. The grand entryway was filled with light reflecting off the chandelier in the high ceiling, and a beautiful rug led up to the antique front desk. The walls were decorated with art that she wanted to get a closer look at—she had the feeling that there were a lot of little details that Angela had included when she'd created the inn's new look. As an interior designer, that was definitely her forte.

The entire place was even nicer than Grace had remembered, and it had already been one of the most beautiful places she'd ever seen when she was younger.

"Hi, welcome to the Beachside Inn!" The woman behind the desk greeted her with a smile and a small wave. Her hair was a bright, vibrant red that suited her complexion perfectly, and she wore several bangle bracelets on each wrist.

"Hi!" Grace walked up, still unable to tear her eyes away from the newly renovated space. "I'm Grace Nelson."

"Oh, Grace! It's so good to meet you! I've heard so many good things. I'm Kathy." The bubbly young woman stood and shook Grace's hand, her bracelets jangling loudly. "Lydia and Angela are super excited to see you."

"Grace?" Angela's head appeared in a doorway, and her face lit up when she locked eyes with Grace. "Ah! You're finally here!"

The two women hugged, and before Grace could recover from the impact, she was wrapped in a hug from Lydia too.

"You guys look so amazing!" Grace said, studying her old friends.

And she wasn't just trying to flatter them—they really did look great. It wasn't just how they were aging, although they looked good in that sense too. If they'd been strangers, she wouldn't have guessed they were the ages they were, creeping up on forty just like she was.

She could hardly believe how different, yet the same, both Angela and Lydia looked. Angela's warm blonde hair just brushed her shoulders in a classic but stylish cut, and her blue eyes were still bright with happiness. Lydia's jade colored eyes sparkled in a similar way, and her brown hair was up in a bun, almost as if she hadn't changed it since the last time they had seen one another. They looked so vital and alive, so happy.

"You look great too!" Lydia squeezed Grace's upper arms.

"Thanks," Grace said, even though she didn't feel like she looked all that nice.

Caring for her father had been her number one priority for a long time, not her appearance. Her dark hair wasn't cut in any particular style, and she hadn't worn much makeup since her father's funeral. Although she'd had a lot of fun going shopping in preparation for her arrival in Marigold, she felt a little washed out and frumpy, even in her brand new clothes. It was taking a while for her to get back into the way her life had been before her father had fallen ill.

"The inn looks incredible too," Grace added, shaking off her negative thoughts. "I can't believe you both did this!"

"We had a ton of help, trust me," Angela assured her. "My parents and siblings were here every other day, as was Grant, Lydia's new fiancé."

"Wow. The last time I saw Travis and Brooke, they were driving you nuts," Grace said, smiling at the last memory she had of each of Angela's siblings. Back then, Brooke had been eleven with a mouthful of braces, and Travis had just been becoming a teenager, awkward phase and all.

"Oh, that hasn't changed." Angela laughed. "But they're much more helpful now. We've mentioned Brooke's bakery, right? She makes the pastries for the inn every day."

"They're so divine," Kathy added with a dreamy sigh. She lifted a brow at Grace. "Want me to go grab us all something from the kitchen?"

"That would be amazing, if it's not too much trouble," Grace said. She had only eaten an overpriced banana and protein bar during her layover at the airport in Boston. "Something small would be fantastic."

"It's not any trouble at all, especially since I'm in the mood for a little pick me up too. Be right back." Kathy disappeared down the hall.

"Let's get you checked in," Lydia said, stepping behind the desk and sitting down at the computer.

Lydia efficiently checked Grace in, giving her a substantial discount, and Kathy returned with a few mini scones on a little plate. Grace thanked her and took a bite. A creamy cinnamon flavor exploded over her tongue, and she almost groaned at how good it tasted. It had been a long time since she'd had anything that delicious.

Once Grace finished her scone—which didn't take long at all—Angela and Lydia took her up to her room. It had an amazing view, looking out onto the ocean with trees on either side, almost like a frame. The cream-colored walls and ivory sheets made it feel almost spa-like. Exactly what she needed.

"We'll leave you to get settled for a bit," Angela told her. "Then do you want to get something to eat beyond a little scone?"

"Definitely." Grace put her bag down and unzipped it.

Angela and Lydia left Grace to unpack. She dug out her essentials, including her toiletries, and put them in the bathroom, then pulled out the small container with her father's ashes. She put the urn on the dark wooden dresser next to a decorative bowl. He had loved the inn and Marigold in general, and Grace wished he could have seen the inn in its restored glory.

She looked at the ashes for another few moments before digging back into her bag. She wanted to visit a few of their old special places and scatter his ashes in the ocean while she was here. The thought of doing so created that sad ache in her chest again, making her rub the spot absently. She shook herself out of her thoughts and headed back downstairs.

"Ready to go?" Lydia asked.

"Yup, definitely! I'm excited to try this amazing

food you guys have been talking about non-stop," Grace said, smiling.

They said goodbye to Kathy and headed out to downtown Marigold. Grace had seen parts of it on her drive in, but parking on the edge and wandering through it made her realize just how much the town had changed.

It still had the same small-town feeling, but updated. Much like the inn, a lot of the buildings had gotten a fresh coat of paint and updated signs. There was almost everything that she'd had back in Colorado, including a yoga studio.

The restaurant they chose served the exact things that Grace was craving—something delicious and summery that would hit just the right spot. The menu was an interesting mashup of New England classics and Mexican food, so she picked a Mexican-inspired lobster roll with chips. Angela and Lydia promised to share some of their tacos.

"To reunions?" Grace asked, lifting her glass of white wine.

"To reunions!" Lydia and Angela said, clinking their glasses against Grace's.

The food hadn't even arrived yet, but Grace felt oddly satisfied nonetheless. It had been a while since she'd been able to enjoy a glass of wine, much less a glass of wine in the middle of the afternoon. And when was the last time she had gone out to a completely new restaurant? Ages. The view was also nice, looking out onto a small clearing where a few people had started a community garden. The spot felt oddly familiar.

"Did a bike shop used to be here back when we were teenagers?" Grace asked.

"I think so, yeah." Angela paused, thinking about it. "No, that used to be next door, but they moved one block over. This used to be a different restaurant."

"Ah, right."

Just like Grace had, Angela had grown up on Marigold Island, and had only returned in the last year or so after living in Philadelphia for a while. She knew the town backward and forward.

"This was that old sandwich place," Lydia added. "The one where all the kids who went to your school worked during the summer."

"Right!" The memories came flooding back into Grace's mind. "The place where the guy Rachel had a crush on worked. The one with that sad little mustache. Otto, or something?"

"Oh god, I forgot about him. Yeah, his name was Otto." Angela snorted. "Remember that time we snuck out to the bonfire he had toward the end of one summer? I think we were sixteen or so."

"Yes! That wasn't worth the lecture I got from my parents after." Lydia smiled wryly at the memory, swirling her wine in her glass.

"I managed not to get caught. I'm not sure how," Angela commented with a touch of pride in her voice. "But I agree—the party was definitely overhyped."

"Way, way overhyped. But at least Rachel kissed Otto at the end of the night," Grace said. "So it was worth it for her."

"I miss her," Lydia said. "It would have been great to have her here for this little reunion too."

"Yeah. How is she? I haven't had the chance to catch up with her in a while," Angela said. "Besides social media, which isn't really the same."

"She's good, or so I've heard. She's still living in Chicago with her daughter and husband," Lydia said.

"Oh, that's nice. Chicago's a great city," Grace said. "And speaking of husbands, congratulations on your engagement, Lydia!"

"Thank you!" Lydia's cheeks flushed and her eyes lit up. "It's still a little surreal. I can't believe that Grant and I found each other, much less the fact that we're getting married."

Grace had to smile at the glow in her friend's face. When Lydia had told her the story of how she and Grant had found each other and fallen in love, she'd felt warm inside. It was the kind of story she loved to read about or watch in a movie.

"Love works in mysterious ways." Angela grinned. "Are you seeing anyone, Grace?"

"Goodness, no." Grace laughed. "I wasn't sure if I could juggle caring for Dad, making sure he was okay, and dating someone, so it's been a while since I've even been out like that. Plus, I don't know how I feel about online dating, and I'm *so* not a bar person. I think I'm a few years past that."

"I see." Lydia said as she looked at Angela in a way that Grace easily recognized. She had seen it time and time again when they were younger, usually right before they'd done something that would get them in a little trouble.

Grace burst out laughing, narrowing her eyes a little. "What are you two plotting?"

"How did you know we were plotting anything?" Lydia asked, laughing along.

"Because you look just like you did when we

were in high school. Like something was afoot." Grace snorted.

"Well, true." Angela shrugged, picking up her napkin and spreading it over her lap. "We were thinking about setting you up with someone. Just to get you back on the horse."

Grace paused as the waiter dropped off their food, giving her time to think. Her thoughts were interrupted when she finally tasted the lobster roll. It was perfect—the hint of spice and cilantro went surprisingly well with the lobster.

"That good, huh?" Lydia asked.

Grace could only nod and give a thumbs up. They all took a few moments to eat a few bites before speaking again.

"But anyway, what do you think about being set up?" Angela asked.

"I have someone in mind." Lydia glanced at Angela again, that same mischievous look in her eyes as before. Angela raised an eyebrow in question, and Lydia answered, "I'm thinking of Cap."

"Oh! Yes! How did we not think about him before?" Angela sat back in her seat. "The Captain would be perfect."

"I have no idea who that is, and thanks for the

offer, but I'm not really interested in dating right now," Grace said with a chuckle. "Maybe you guys can put your matchmaking skills to work with someone else."

* * *

Angela's stomach was still pleasantly full by the time they got back to the inn that evening. Grace headed upstairs to get settled into her room for the night, so Angela and Lydia walked over to the innkeeper's residence.

When they walked in, they found Brooke in the living room on the couch, watching a TV show on low volume. She had been babysitting Angela's son Jake while they were out and hadn't minded spending a little more time with him while Angela caught up with Grace.

"Hey, Jake's in bed already," Brooke said when the two other women came into the room.

"Thanks, you're a lifesaver. How was everything?" Angela asked, picking up a drawing of a dinosaur that was on the coffee table. She smiled and decided to put it up on the fridge.

"Good!" Brooke got to her feet, tucking some of her light blonde hair behind her ear. "We ate, drew some stuff, and watched a little TV. How were things with Grace?"

"It was so much fun," Lydia said. "After we finished eating, we had to hit up the Sweet Creamery for ice cream and walked on the beach while we ate it. It was so nice to catch up."

"Yeah, it was just as if no time had passed at all." Angela sat down next to Brooke. Her feet were already getting a bit sore from walking barefoot on the sand. "I think Grace felt the same way. Her spirits seemed even higher by the time we got back."

"I think so too. I hope this is the fresh start she needs." Lydia perched on the edge of the couch. "I definitely needed one when I showed up here."

"It's like what we talked about a while back," Angela said. "The Beachside Inn can be a place of second chances and new beginnings."

"Yeah." Lydia smiled gently, as did Brooke. "I love that idea. I hope Grace finds hope and healing here, just like we did."

CHAPTER THREE

Joshua Marsden had his first cup of coffee before he did anything else, shuffling from his bedroom to his kitchen to hit the button to get the first pot brewing. Once he had enough caffeine in his system to function, he was able to check his emails, which he worked through while drinking his second cup—always taken black. Then he got ready for yet another hectic day.

Today, he took a long drink of his third cup of coffee of the day with just a touch of heavy cream as he walked through the back door of his restaurant, Ariana. It was more or less his second home. His baby. He had built it up with a lot of hard work and sleepless nights to make it one of Marigold's most popular restaurants.

It was barely eight, so it was fairly quiet both in the kitchen and out in the guest area. Usually, it was bustling with activity—he had several great chefs on his team who didn't mind showing up early, and a dedicated customer base of both tourists and locals who kept him busy.

"Morning, Alan," Joshua said to his head chef and good friend, who was already starting prep for lunch service.

"Morning." Alan's eyes went straight to Joshua's coffee cup. "What number are you on?"

"Why does it matter?" Joshua asked, holding his to-go cup close as if Alan was going to snatch it away. "It's pretty much part of my blood at this point, so who cares if it's the third or fourth?"

Alan laughed, putting some diced tomatoes into a container for later. "Because some days, I think that caffeine is the only thing keeping you up and about."

"Hey! The coffee's just an added boost to my already high levels of energy," Joshua insisted. "Energy I need to get through the hectic day. So, how's prep going?"

"Good. We got that fish shipment right on time, so today's special is good to go," Alan said, going to wash his hands. "And the line cooks are coming in about fifteen minutes to finish up the prep."

"You got the extra pecorino, right?" Joshua asked, going through his to-do list on his phone. It looked endless, but then again, it felt like the work never really finished when you were running a restaurant. "It seems like every dish that includes it is selling like crazy."

"Yup." Alan pulled a pad of paper and a pen from his pocket, looking over his to-do's as well. That was part of the reason why Joshua trusted him—he cared just as much about Ariana as Joshua did.

"Good." Joshua leaned up against the wall, running a hand through his dark brown hair. There were bits of gray at his temples, silver strands that had appeared slowly over the last couple years. "I should be in and out throughout lunch service. I have a few calls lined up for the possible new locations."

Since Ariana was incredibly successful, Joshua wanted to expand. He had his eyes on Boston first, since the buzz about the restaurant outside of the island was mostly concentrated in that area, then maybe another big city. Philadelphia seemed like a solid bet, and maybe New York if things went well. It was a lot of work—some days, it felt like he woke up and worked right up until he passed out again at the end of the day—but the payoff seemed promising. More locations would mean more recognition, more money, and potentially some big awards.

"So you're basically not going to sit down at all today?" Alan said, raising an eyebrow at him.

"What's the deal with the eyebrow?" Joshua asked, even though he knew exactly what his friend was about to say.

"You know exactly what I'm getting at, man." Alan laughed, pointing his pen at Joshua. "You're going to either work yourself to the bone or drink all of Marigold's coffee trying. You need to at least sit down for a minute. Take a breather. Take a little downtime."

"I'm fine." Joshua tucked his phone into the back pocket of his well-worn jeans. Being the boss meant he didn't have to wear anything fussy if he didn't want to. "I thrive off of this. I could take a break whenever I want to, but I choose *not* to. I'd drive myself nuts with a full day off."

"Mm-hm." Alan glanced at the door as two line cooks came in, chatting about their weekends. "So you'd take a day off right now? Today?"

"No," Joshua said quickly, sipping his coffee. "I mean, not now. I have meetings and all that."

"So when *would* you take a break?"

Joshua paused, looking Alan in the eye for a few

beats. "I would have to see. I can't look into the future."

"Total cop-out answer."

"It's not!"

"Okay, then. Let's make a bet," Alan said.

"What are the terms?" Joshua couldn't resist anything that felt like a game or competition. He credited his success to his desire to win.

"If you try some new things, take a bit of time off and get out of your comfort zone, I'll buy you a bottle of top shelf whiskey. But if you back out or don't give it a real shot, I win the bet. And if I win, you have to dye your hair orange."

"Done." Joshua extended his hand, but Alan just laughed.

"You didn't even hear the details of the bargain," Alan said. "I'm going to sign you up for a bunch of recreational activities, and you'll have to give them an honest shot. And you won't get to pick any of them or know what they are more than a day ahead of time."

Joshua paused, his hand still in the air as Alan put his out for him to shake. What harm could a little bet do?

"I'm still in," Joshua said, shaking Alan's hand with a firm grip.

*　*　*

Grace put on some comfortable shoes, grabbed her camera bag, and headed out to explore Marigold on foot. It was another gorgeous day, and even with the amazing view of the water and the steady breeze from her open window, she couldn't bear to be inside for another minute.

The walk from the inn to the edge of town didn't take long. She remembered the path easily since she, Lydia, Angela, and Rachel had walked it many times in their teenage days, although things looked a bit different now. The shops were much more modern, and the variety was even better on this side of town. She made a mental note of the places she wanted to try out before walking toward the beach again—a craft shop, a place that sold fancy soaps, and a pizza place that smelled so good that she almost stopped to get a slice.

She arrived at a small beachfront path, grateful that the spot hadn't changed. This was the place where her dad had taught her how to ride a bike, and they had ridden there throughout her childhood. Every scraped knee and bruise had been worth the feeling of riding quickly down a hill, the wind against her face and her father's laughter close by.

They had walked here too, eating ice cream from the old shop that had been the Sweet Creamery's only real competition on the island. She missed talking to him. Since it had been just the two of them for most of her life, they had formed a special bond where she felt like she could talk to him about a lot of things. That was something she'd missed the most when he'd gotten really sick.

She walked along the path, taking in the scenery a bit before finding the perfect place to take a photo—she had a great view of the water, and beyond it, the other side of the island. After she snapped a photo, she walked a little more before taking another in the direction she had just come from. The inn was a small dot in the distance at this point.

Grace paused after taking a photo of a flock of birds, thinking back to dinner with Lydia and Angela. She had said she hadn't had a lot of time for herself lately, which was completely true. Her "me time" had usually been spent eating ice cream on the couch, then passing out there until she woke up with a start, wondering if she'd given her dad his evening medications. She always had, but she'd still worried like crazy.

She sighed. Besides photography, she had no idea what "me time" would look like anymore.

Reading more was definitely on the list, as was catching up on all the TV that she'd missed. But those were small in the big scheme of things. She wanted to really do something out of her comfort zone—something that would break her out of the shell she had been in for so long.

Some other scenery caught her eye as she walked, and she turned back into town. A slice of pizza sounded nice after all. Even though she'd had an amazing muffin with some fruit for breakfast, wandering around for an hour or two had made her work up an appetite. She found the pizza place again and got a big slice of pepperoni pizza. The front windows were open, so she chose a spot on a stool next to it.

There was a big bulletin board a few feet to her left, which she looked over as she ate. A few teenagers had put up ads for their babysitting services, as she once had to earn a little spending money, and many people were trying to sell things. But a neon pink flyer caught her eye above everything else.

It read, *Want to learn something new? Try out a class today!*

She got up and took a closer look, bringing her slice with her. Marigold's rec center had classes for adults in a number of areas, from pottery to birdwatching to "fun and funky needlepoint," whatever that meant. Her face lit up, a grin stretching her lips. This was exactly what she needed. In order to find out what her time to herself would look like, she had to try something different, something she hadn't thought of doing before.

There was more on their website, which she pulled up on her phone. The list was even longer online. Since it was the summer, there were a lot of classes coming up soon. Just from eyeballing it, more than half were way out of her comfort zone and many of them piqued her curiosity.

Perfect.

She finished up her pizza slice as she made a list of the activities that interested her the most, then headed back to the inn feeling refreshed.

CHAPTER FOUR

Brooke's frequent walks with Angela on the beach were one of her favorite ways to relax and recharge, especially with the summer weather. Now they could take their shoes off and walk on the water's edge, letting the tide sweep over their feet. It was incredibly soothing. At her bakery, she was on her feet all day, and even just the slightest bit of sea water on her skin helped the ache.

"How are things with Patrick?" Brooke asked. "It's been a while since I've seen him."

She missed seeing Patrick Devlin at their family dinners or on double dates when he and Angela would meet up with Brooke and her boyfriend, Hunter. Patrick and Angela were a perfect match for each other—he was kind, funny, attentive, and great with Jake. He was a far cry from Scott, Angela's ex-husband.

"Things are great! He's just been tied up with his book's upcoming release and all the things he has to do to prepare for it," Angela said. "He's a bit nervous, even though it's an amazing book."

"I totally get that." Brooke chuckled and kicked at the wet sand. "He's put in all that hard work and waited so long. It would be crushing to not have everything go the way you want it to."

"Exactly. He's already gotten good reviews from a few prominent critics, so he's feeling a little bit better. Emphasis on a little bit."

"He doesn't think the book is good?" Brooke asked. She had read an early copy and thought it was phenomenal. It was one of those books that she'd had to stay up late to finish even though she'd had to wake up as early as she always did the next day.

"No, he likes it a lot and thinks it's some of his best work. I think it's just the feeling of having this project one hundred percent out of his hands now that it's about to be released to the public. I doubt those nerves or self-doubt will ever go away, even after publishing a few more bestsellers. Plus, it's sort of like peach pie—you might make the best one in the world, and someone just might not like peaches."

"Hey, my peach pie could convert even the biggest peach hater," Brooke said with a laugh. "But as his book starts getting press and stuff, is his anxiety getting better or worse?"

"It's definitely getting more intense. He's told me all about his pre-publication fears, so I know he'll calm down when it's finally out there for the world to read." Angela's smile softened with warmth. "I'm glad he's sharing this whole experience with me. It's kind of like I'm getting a peek into the inner workings of his brain."

"And clearly, you like what you see in there."

"I do. I love everything about him. His sweet side, his worries, all of it." Angela shrugged. "It's so funny. Back in high school, I was too nervous to even talk to him because he seemed so cool and nice and put together. Well, as put together as a high-schooler can be. But he's human just like everyone else, and that's what makes him special to me."

Brooke nodded, understanding her sister's words completely. Hunter Reed was a movie star, but very few of the interviews and articles on him were even close to capturing the real man—the one who loved cheesy movies just as much as he loved award-winning documentaries, and who had goofy conversations with their cat, Scratch, as if the dark-haired kitten were a little person.

"I'm glad I made the leap," Angela added. "I thought it was way too soon to date after the divorce, but it was the right choice. I can't imagine where I'd be without him now. He made me realize just how much I was missing in life with Scott."

"Speaking of jumping into a new relationship too soon, how is Scott doing now that his engagement's been called off?" Brooke asked.

After hearing a bit about Scott's ex, Brooke hadn't been surprised when Angela had told her that Scott had called off his engagement. Angela hadn't been a big fan of his ex-fiancée's influence on Jake, so at least her sister wouldn't have to worry about that anymore.

"Oof, I'm not totally sure. He seemed super down about it when he told me, naturally, but he seems to be in better spirits now when we video chat with Jake. He's been dating again since he split with Cheryl, but nothing's gotten serious." Angela sighed. "I think it's for the best. He definitely needs some time to sort himself out before he dates again."

The two walked in comfortable silence for a while, and Brooke's thoughts drifted to her relationship with Hunter. Marigold felt like a safe bubble in some ways. Once the novelty of a well-known actor living in the small town wore off, the locals didn't come up to him all that much. With the influx of tourists for the summer, he got stopped on the street a little more, but not that often. It almost made her forget he was famous until something from outside the bubble popped into her life.

"Did you know I was in a tabloid the other day?" Brooke asked, glancing at her sister.

"What? Seriously?"

"Yeah. It was just a picture of us walking around in downtown Marigold. They didn't have anything mean to say, but it was still a little weird."

"I bet," Angela said. "What *did* they have to say?"

"Just that I was his girlfriend and that I was a 'small business owner.' I kind of wish they'd put the bakery's name out there, but it's already doing so well that I'm not sure if I need that kind of exposure." Brooke shrugged, then grimaced. "I looked like a total mess in the photo they published, though. I was in leggings and a t-shirt from the bakery with my clogs on, my hair up in a messy bun. It was mostly a baking day, so I wasn't going to get dolled up."

"I'm sure you looked fine."

"Thanks for the vote of confidence, but I strongly disagree. I've definitely looked better." Brooke laughed. "I doubt there'll be many more pics like that, though. Hunter is pretty much done with the Hollywood scene. And he's making a turn toward more serious roles too. I mean, I might still appear in a tabloid somewhere, but I hope it doesn't become a big thing. I'll have to figure out how to navigate that if and when the time comes."

"That sounds a little scary." Angela's expression turned concerned.

"A little bit, but if I have to look like a tired mess on *Us Weekly's* website, then that's just how it's going to be. Hunter is completely worth it." Brooke laughed, her smile widening. "I've never been happier with anyone else. Or happier, period. My business is going well, I'm dating the man of my dreams, and I get to hang out with you more."

Brooke looped her arm in Angela's and gave her a squeeze. Both of them couldn't keep the smiles off their faces as they continued their walk along the beach.

* * *

Grace patted her purse, double-checking that she had everything she needed for the day, then headed downstairs for breakfast with a bounce in her step. Today was her first day of her plan to try as many new things as she could, but first she had to fuel up.

"Hey, Kathy!" Grace greeted the red-headed woman, swinging by the front desk.

"Good morning!" Kathy looked up from the computer. "Heading to breakfast?"

"Yup. I have a full day ahead of me." Grace peeked at what Kathy was eating. "What's the pastry of the day?"

"Wild berry scones." Kathy held up her half-eaten treat. "So good."

"I wouldn't expect anything less." Grace grinned.

In the short time she had been staying at the Beachside Inn, she had gotten addicted to Brooke's pastries. She hadn't tasted such moist, yet crumbly scones in her life. And the muffins... She'd had to have one every day. They managed to be just sweet enough to feel like a treat, but not so sweet that she felt like she'd had dessert for breakfast. There hadn't been a single thing that had disappointed her yet.

"The wild berry scones are a hit, Brooke," Kathy called, looking past Grace.

"Really?" Brooke asked, stepping into the inn with Angela behind her. "I'm so glad! I tweaked the recipe a little bit. The berries are from a local farm. And good morning, Grace!"

"Good morning to you guys too. Excuse me while I go taste one of these scones myself."

Grace headed into the common area, where the scones and other pastries were calling her name. There were other guests having their breakfast there too, sipping tea and coffee while discussing their plans for the day. Grace spotted Lydia talking to one of them and waved hello to her as well.

There was a full spread of scones, muffins, bagels, and danishes, such a great spread that Grace couldn't decide on what to go for first. Ultimately, she chose two scones—one wild berry, one cherry and marzipan. With her requisite cup of coffee with cream and sugar, she settled into one of the window seats to enjoy her breakfast.

"Hey, what are you up to today?" Lydia asked, coming to stand next to the window seat across from Grace with a mug of coffee.

"I have my first class in a bit at the rec center. A pottery class," Grace told her. "I'm a little nervous."

"Don't be. It sounds fun!" Lydia smiled. "Also, you're an artist already. So you're probably way more prepared for a class like this than most people."

Grace snorted. "There's a huge difference between taking an interesting photo and creating a piece of art with my bare hands."

"Well, you'll have the artistic vision, and that seems like half the battle." Lydia sipped her coffee.

"Ever the optimist."

"I try." Lydia's smile returned. "And if it's not something you're into, it's just one day—so no harm, no foul. And then you can check that off of your list of potential hobbies."

"Yeah, true." Grace smiled too. Despite her apprehension, she was really looking forward to trying some new things.

"I've got to head into the back to handle some emails. Tell me all about it later tonight?" Lydia checked her watch before glancing back up at her friend.

"Yes, definitely!"

Grace quickly finished up her breakfast, then headed out to the rec center in her rental car, nerves bubbling in her belly the entire way. She tried to keep Lydia's words in mind. If this didn't work out, she could move onto the next thing. That was the whole point of this—to eliminate things one by one until she found something that would be a good way to fill her new "me time."

Once she arrived and found a parking spot, Grace followed the rec center's signs to the pottery room, which had a row of wheels along either side of the narrow portion of the room. On the side of the room opposite the door, it opened up into a bigger space with industrial shelving lining the walls. There were already pieces of pottery resting there, creations that looked much better than Grace knew hers would be.

She took a seat at one of the wheels, just as the other few people who were already there had. Slowly but surely, more people trickled in until there were ten others. There were adults of various ages but all of them seemed more comfortable and at ease in the pottery studio than she did.

Well, except for the man who had sat next to her, who came in last. He looked a little lost and nervous too, his dark hair a bit disheveled as if he'd run his hands through it on the way in. There was a little gray hair coming in at his temples, so Grace figured he was a few years older than her, maybe in his early forties.

She fiddled around with the pottery wheel in front of her, trying not to look at him too much. He was one of the most handsome men she had seen in a while. Now that he was sitting next to her, she could take in the strong angle of his jaw and the light stubble along it. She liked his style too—his jeans looked well-loved, and he was wearing a simple t-shirt with a faded, vintage Coca Cola logo on it.

He tentatively touched the wheel just like she was doing, as if he was making sure it wasn't going to blow up on him. Grace had to smile a little, her shoulders relaxing. At least she wasn't the only one feeling like she was completely out of her element.

CHAPTER FIVE

Joshua looked around at the other people in his pottery class. *This* was the first thing Alan had chosen for him to do? Well, his friend had done a good job of picking something that was totally out of Joshua's comfort zone. Joshua could cook pretty much anything in a pot, but *making* said pot was a whole different story.

The last time he'd tried something visually artistic—except plating a dish to look as beautiful as possible—had been way back in college when he'd taken a mandatory visual arts class. It hadn't gone well at all. He was still sure that his professor gave him a B- just because he'd showed up every time.

The instructor of today's lesson, an older man

wearing a paint-stained t-shirt and old jeans, stood up to address the class.

"Welcome to this introduction to pottery course," the man said with a smile. "I'm Gerald, your instructor for the day. By the time you leave, you'll each have made your first pots and gotten a general understanding of the art of pottery. Let's head over to the clay area to start."

Gerald motioned for everyone to follow him to the larger part of the room, which they did. He gave them a mini-tour of the facilities first before they stopped in front of a wall of finished pieces. As the instructor explained the basic principles of pottery and how the process from raw clay to finished product worked, Joshua split his attention between him and the pretty, dark-haired woman who he had been sitting next to before class started.

Her hair was up in a ponytail and she was dressed casually, like he was. She had lovely hazel eyes that he wanted to see more of, but he didn't want to get caught staring at her. He turned his focus back to Gerald, although it took a little effort.

"Now, what do you all know about clay?" Gerald asked the class.

"Next to nothing besides the fact that I tried to eat it as a kid. That definitely didn't work out,"

Joshua murmured. The dark-haired woman snorted, as did a few others.

"And that's exactly why they make non-toxic clay for kids," Gerald replied with a laugh. "The best way to get to know clay is to work with it, so I'll get all of you set-up. You can return to your wheels now."

Joshua sat back at the wheel he'd been settled at before, and the dark-haired woman took her seat next to him again. Gerald put buckets of wet clay in front of everyone so they would share with the person next to them.

"Let's start with the mechanics of the wheel," Gerald said, taking a seat at his wheel.

Joshua watched as the older man demonstrated how to work the wheel and a ball of clay, one eyebrow drifting up higher and higher as Gerald easily manipulated the ball into a column, then back into a ball, then into a beautiful-looking bowl shape. He might as well have done a magic trick in Joshua's eyes.

"Go ahead and play around with it a little bit—just get a feel of how the clay works in your hands. Don't worry about trying to make anything pretty. There's slip if you need to re-wet your clay, just like I did," Gerald said, standing up.

Joshua started the wheel up and watched his ball of clay turn around and around. He rested his hands on it, feeling its shape warp immediately into something lumpy and odd-looking. It had been a long time since he'd felt so awkward doing something with his hands, almost like he had when he first started learning how to cook as a teenager. The knives had felt unwieldy, and he'd had no idea how to make anything beyond noodles.

"I feel like he just explained how to drive a stick-shift when I've never seen a car in my life," Joshua said.

"Really?" the dark-haired woman looked over at what he was doing. "It's not so bad. The ball you've got going there makes it seem like you've at least *seen* a car before, to steal your metaphor."

"Well, thanks." Joshua snorted and looked over at her work. She had created a small bowl-shaped object that also looked lumpy and a little sad, but it was almost like high art compared to what he had created. "Gerald said that we weren't supposed to try to make anything pretty, yet here you are."

The woman looked at him face-on, surprised. Her eyes were an even lovelier shade of hazel than he'd thought, her pupil surrounded by a dark, almost gray shade that spread out into a lighter greenish color toward the outside of her irises.

"Wait, you're talking to me?" she asked.

"Yeah."

The woman laughed, shaking her head. "I beg to differ. I feel like a cavewoman who just discovered what clay is for the very first time. Maybe I'll end up making something in the shape of an antelope or whatever they hunted back then."

Joshua grinned at her quick response. He always appreciated a sharp wit. Before he could say anything else, Gerald made his way back to the front of the room.

"Okay, great work so far," the instructor said, sinking down behind his wheel again. "Now let's work with a few detailing tools. These can create texture in your work."

Gerald walked them through using little tools to add hatch marks and lines in their clay, then set them off to play around for a while and get comfortable with the process.

"Are you making that antelope?" Joshua asked, spinning his wheel as he held a pointed tool lightly against his clay ball.

"Nope, I think I'm going to graduate on to a bowl with antelopes etched into the side." The woman looked up at him, humor in her eyes. "What about you?"

"I'll just see where the clay guides me." Joshua stopped his wheel and looked at what he'd created. The pointed tool had created a deeper gouge than he'd intended, making it look like he was trying to make a hole in his pot. "Too bad my clay has a terrible sense of direction."

The woman laughed again. "I don't know—maybe it's trying to take the road less traveled."

"Maybe." His smile broadened. "I'm Joshua, by the way."

"I'm Grace." She extended a clay-covered hand to him, which he shook. "Nice to meet you."

Grace, he thought. It was a fitting name. Even though she seemed warm and down to earth, something about the way she sat was graceful.

"All right, now it's time to finally turn those shapeless balls into a vase!" Gerald said enthusiastically. "Eyes up here, please."

Once he had everyone's attention, the instructor showed them how to start making a pot, as well as the ways to change up the shape to be wider or narrower, patch up any holes, or shore up the sides so they wouldn't collapse in on themselves. Once his demonstration was done, he turned on a classic rock station and left them to their own devices.

Joshua had no idea what kind of pot he wanted to make. He wasn't even sure if he had a use for a decorative pot at home. But this was just for fun, so he decided to let whatever happened, happen.

"What are you going to use your pot for?" Grace asked in a low voice.

"That's assuming I'm going to get anything useful out of this," Joshua said with a laugh. "I don't think a pot that let all the water out would be good."

"Well, assuming you did get something useful out of it, what would you use it for?"

"A cautionary tale of what happens when I attempt to make pottery." Joshua tried to build up the sides, but they collapsed in on themselves. "What about you?"

"Probably the same. Maybe something for flowers, although they might have to be fake ones, since I don't trust the sides of this thing." Grace tilted her head a bit and slowed down her wheel. "I wonder if keeping the sides low will make it sturdier."

"Seems like sound logic."

The two of them worked quietly, the sounds of other students chatting and the music playing in the background. Joshua had to admit that he was having fun. It was nice working with his hands in a new way, even if it wasn't going to produce anything of value.

"Ah, I finally got it to be tall!" Grace said, slowing down her wheel. Her vase was about six inches high. "It just needed more clay, which seems super obvious now."

"It looks good!" Joshua looked between her piece and his, picking up an etching tool. "I think mine might end up being useful, somehow."

"Yeah, it already looks cool." She glanced at his work again.

Joshua slowed down his wheel, and as he did, the vase went a little bit lopsided. He winced. "Huh. Let's just say it's abstract?"

"Sure, abstract." Grace smiled. She had a great smile too—it made her eyes twinkle.

They chatted off and on about their projects as the class went on, and by the end, they each had a passable vase. Grace's still had the height she liked, but the texture she'd added on the outside was uneven. Joshua had created something half that height, and no matter how hard he tried, it was still a little bit lopsided. Even so, he felt a little bubble of pride that he'd managed to create anything at all.

"This might not have to be buried deep in my closet," he said, holding up his piece.

"I'm telling you, it's just abstract. If you painted it, you could pass it off as something fancy and pretentious." Grace looked at her piece. "I don't think mine will be shoved in the closet either."

"Yeah, it's not bad at all," he assured her.

Gerald showed them where to put their creations so that the pots could be fired and sealed. They would be ready to pick up in a few days. After the class officially ended, everyone started to file out to the parking lot, and Grace and Joshua followed suit. As Grace dug through her purse for her keys, he thought about asking for her number.

She was beautiful, of course, but that wasn't the only reason he was considering it. It had been a while since he'd joked around with a woman the way he had with her. He didn't date much, but he knew that being able to banter and joke around with someone was something he wanted. Nothing was worse than an awkward date filled with long, empty pauses and misunderstood jokes.

But before he could say anything to her, his phone rang, and he dug it out of his pocket and glanced at the screen. It was Alan. Slipping immediately back into business mode, Joshua waved goodbye to Grace and answered it.

Work couldn't wait.

* * *

Lydia loved cooking in Grant's kitchen. It was a little bigger than hers, and the appliances were newer, but most importantly, he was always there. She looked down at her ring as she chopped up some herbs. The diamonds caught in the sunlight streaming in from the window above the sink, making her pause for a moment before she dumped the herbs into their salad.

Grant noticed what she was looking at and lifted her left hand to gently kiss the back of it. Lydia smiled at him as he held on to her hand, looking at the ring as well.

"I was so nervous when I proposed," he murmured, stroking the underside of her wrist.

"Really?" Lydia asked. "Were you afraid I'd say no?"

"No, not at all. I don't think I would've asked if I hadn't felt sure we were on the same page. But it was still a little nerve-racking." He laced his fingers through hers and let their joined hands drop between them. "There was the planning aspect of it—you have no idea how much I had to scramble with the DJ and the signs. It all seemed so easy on paper, but I was flubbing everything from nerves."

"Seriously?" Lydia laughed. "I wouldn't have guessed it. It all went off so perfectly to me."

"Well, that's great to hear." He squeezed her hand. "But I was mostly nervous because I never expected to ask someone to marry me again. And I never *want* to ask that question again for the rest of my life."

He dropped his head and gave Lydia a kiss. His kisses still made her knees feel a little weak, so she leaned into him. When their kiss broke, she rested her head on his chest, taking in the steady sound of his heartbeat. She loved it when Grant got soft with her. Most of the island never would have guessed he had it in him if they just saw him managing his employees at his landscaping business or walking around town. He had a gruff exterior, but there was so much more than that beneath the surface.

"Well, you won't have to," Lydia promised him, going back to cooking. "I don't plan on going anywhere. Speaking of marriage stuff, what do you want to do for the wedding?"

They hadn't really put any plans into action yet

—they were just enjoying being engaged. Neither of them had really taken the time to enjoy this stage before, so they were taking it easy now.

"Something on the smaller side, definitely."

"Agreed." Lydia nodded. "Something intimate and romantic with just a few of our closest friends?"

"Exactly like that." Grant pulled some rolls out of the oven and put them on a trivet. "How's the fall sound?"

Lydia grinned. Images of the perfect small celebration with Marigold in its full fall glory filled her head. The trees behind the inn were incredible during that season, and with the mix between the changing leaves and the beautiful ocean out back, it would be picture perfect. Autumn wasn't too far from now, especially when it came to planning a wedding in that time, but she got the feeling that Grant didn't want to wait to tie the knot either. They were both enjoying being engaged, but it would be even better when she could call him her husband.

"It sounds perfect to me," she murmured.

CHAPTER SIX

Grace woke up early without an alarm, as she'd been doing ever since she'd come to Marigold. Her sleep had been incredibly restful the whole time she'd been here, especially with the calmness outside and the distant sound of the waves in the distance. The sun was just rising, and she felt the perfect, slightly cool breeze coming in from her window. It was the perfect temperature for a jog.

She got dressed and headed out to the beach, walking for a while to warm up before breaking into a slow run. The sand was getting kicked up into her shoes, but she didn't mind. It was nice to wake up and do whatever she wanted to do first and foremost.

She had spent the past decade or so neglecting her own needs and interests, so something as simple as a run on the beach felt almost indulgent. When she'd been caring for her dad, the mornings had always been a tightly controlled routine of medications and appointments that she never deviated from. She'd even eaten the same breakfast every day—oatmeal with peanut butter and raisins. It wasn't nearly as exciting or delicious as one of Brooke's pastries.

Her mind wandered to the list of things she liked to do that were just for her, something she had started in a little notebook that she kept next to her bed at her room in the inn. It was getting longer and longer each day. She made a mental note to add "beachfront runs" to the list when she got back.

She picked up the pace as she went up a bluff, feeling out of breath by the time she got to the top. Slowing to a walk, she took a moment to look out onto the ocean. It was a gorgeous view. The sun was hitting the water just right, and she could see a few small islands off in the distance. A lighthouse on the other side of the island was just at the edge of her field of vision. Marigold Island was situated not far off the coast of Massachusetts, between Martha's Vineyard and Nantucket, and it was known for its picturesque views.

Unfortunately, she didn't have her good camera,

so she snapped a few quick photos with her phone. There was no way she could leave such a beautiful panorama without capturing it in some way. Photography had always been a part of her life, even when her father had been incredibly sick. Usually, it was just a picture on her phone, but sometimes she got the chance to work with her real camera.

Once she got the shots she wanted, she jogged back down the bluff and back toward the inn. By the time she got back, she felt warm and energized for the day.

"Hey, Grace!" Lydia called, waving when Grace passed by the common area.

"Hi!" Grace wandered in, finding Angela and Brooke there too, enjoying a few pastries. "Sorry, I'm a little sweaty and gross."

"Don't worry about it. Want something to eat?" Brooke asked.

"Yes, please. I worked up an appetite." Grace laughed and used the tongs to fill her plate with some fruit and a big blueberry muffin.

"I'm impressed that you actually burned the calories off first," Angela said. "I keep telling myself that I'll run them off after, but 'after' never seems to come."

They all laughed.

"I think I negate all of the health benefits of the run by eating twice as many pastries." Grace broke off a piece of her muffin and popped it into her mouth, letting out a hum of appreciation. It was buttery and just sweet enough. "But I like to think I just end up in a neutral place."

"That's a good way to think about it," Lydia said, sipping her coffee. "What are you up to today?"

"I have another class." Grace put down her plate and poured herself a cup of coffee. "I'll need all the energy I can get for it. Maybe I shouldn't have gone on that run, but it was too pretty out to not go for it."

"What's this one about?" Brooke asked.

"It's an outdoor class. We'll explore the island and learn about the native plants and animals on foot. It's been a long time since I've done anything like this—probably since college—so I figured it would be a good place to start."

"That sounds fun!" Angela said.

"Yeah, I'm loving this little challenge you've set-up for yourself." Lydia gave her a warm smile. "You're really expanding your horizons."

"I'm liking it a lot too." Grace sipped her coffee and smiled. "I can't wait to see how much I learn."

* * *

Joshua adjusted his Bluetooth earpiece as he paced back and forth across his small office, his phone in hand. His call with the developers who would be working on the space that he had his eye on for a new Boston restaurant was starting to drag, and he had to get out his extra energy somehow. There were a number of people on the call, to Joshua's chagrin. It would have been so much more efficient to just talk to one or two people and email everyone else.

"The construction might be a little tough in the winter if you're aiming for a spring launch," someone said.

Joshua ran his hand through his hair. "I factored in delays in my projected timeline."

"Ah, right," the same person said. "But still, you might want to add in more. There might be feet and feet of snow, and people might get sick..."

"I know. Boston winters are pretty brutal, so I want to give the construction team as much time as possible to do their thing." Joshua tried to put a smile into his voice even though all he wanted to do was put his head down on his desk.

"Good, good," someone else said. "So I think that works then. Let's talk about the budget next."

Joshua sat on the edge of his desk as someone talked about the budget and how to coordinate construction so as to not disturb the residents living nearby. He couldn't wait to go to Boston once the planning got further along. He'd even thought about moving there temporarily to be as hands-on as he wanted to be. It would be a big shift from the quiet of Marigold—even some of the calmest neighborhoods in the city couldn't match Marigold on one of its more animated nights—but he was willing to do it.

He had done the same when he'd worked to open Ariana, and it had been extremely worthwhile. Doing the same for this new restaurant sounded like a good path forward. He made a few mental notes about his possible move in his head. First, he'd have to find a place near the construction site. It didn't have to be fancy. And he'd have to figure out what things to move and where to find a renter for his house in Marigold...

He hadn't even started the move and he was already tired.

Joshua sat back behind his desk and put himself on mute as he listened to everyone else talk, opening up his email. It was overflowing with so many messages that he heaved a sigh and ran both hands through his hair. His move checklist would have to wait. Luckily, the call started to wrap up when they all agreed they could take everything offline to tie up loose ends.

Once he hung up, Joshua took out his earpiece and headed out into the kitchen, where Alan and the line chefs were prepping for lunch service.

"What's up? You look like you've just been through the wringer," Alan said, looking up from the list he was checking over.

"Just a call about Boston," Joshua said, sighing again. "And then I looked at my email, and it was out of control. It's going to take forever to get through it all. I don't know how I'm going to fit in my class for today."

"Wow, you're already tapping out on our bet?" Alan asked, a good-natured smirk coming onto his face. "I can't believe it."

Joshua grinned. Alan knew him too well. "Fine, I'll go—even though it probably won't be that exciting. I'll just power through the emails when I get back. I can survive on four hours of sleep."

"That's the spirit."

Joshua checked the time and went to get ready for class, pulling on the hiking shoes he'd brought with him and left in his car. He still couldn't bring himself to get pumped up about it. The pottery class had been a lot of fun because of Grace, and without someone there to chat with and joke around with, he wasn't sure another class would be as enjoyable as the first had been.

Plus, although he liked being outside, he wasn't sure how much he'd use the knowledge of the different plants and animals on the island. He figured that as long as he knew which ones were poisonous or would make him break into a rash and which ones were safe, he was fine.

He drove over to the rec center, where the class was going to meet before heading out on their nature walk, and parked. As he walked toward the group gathered out front, a familiar dark ponytail caught his eye. When the woman turned around, he realized it was Grace.

A smile spread across his face, and he straightened a little.

Maybe this class will be fun after all, he thought.

CHAPTER SEVEN

Grace's eyebrows shot up when she saw Joshua crossing the parking lot, smiling at her and adjusting his dark blue baseball hat.

She waved at him, breaking into a smile, and he waved back. She was happy to see him, although he was the last person she'd expected to sign up for something like this. Even though he had seemed pretty laid back, she couldn't imagine him being outdoorsy enough to do anything beyond a simple hike for pleasure, not searching for plants or animals. He checked in with the instructor, a middle-aged woman whose blonde ponytail was streaked with gray.

"Okay, awesome, I think everyone is here!" the

instructor said. "My name is Marion, and I'll be your guide today. Our first trail isn't too far from here, so please follow me so we can get started."

The group followed her, and Grace drifted toward the back near where Joshua was walking.

"We meet again," he said when she drew up beside him. He smiled at her again, which put a dimple in one of his cheeks that Grace found incredibly endearing. It was a little boyish, a nice contrast to his strong jaw and stubble.

"We do," Grace replied. Then her brows furrowed. "I have to know what made you sign up for this class. It doesn't seem like your style."

He laughed. "It doesn't? Do I give off 'indoors-y' vibes?"

"Mm, a tiny bit. Not indoors-y, necessarily, but not super outdoorsy, if that makes sense. But mostly, I'm just surprised to see you in another class in general." Grace stepped up over a tree root as they headed into a wooded area. "It's a funny coincidence."

"Yeah, my friend Alan actually signed me up for a bunch of classes as part of a bet." He tucked his hands into the pockets of his dark blue pants. "Knowing him, he probably signed me up for whatever was suggested on the website, if there was anything like that."

"Yes, there was," Grace said with a laugh. "I did almost the same thing when I signed up for classes."

"Did one of your friends rope you into a bet too?" He looked at her, amusement in his gray eyes.

"No, I just wanted to try some new things. It's been a long time since I've been able to enjoy the outdoors, and I don't think I've ever learned the name of any plant life beyond maple trees or pine trees."

Marion came to a stop in front of a tree, as did the rest of the group. Everyone fanned out so they could see what she was pointing out. Grace dug into her messenger pack and pulled out a little notepad to take notes.

"Since we're going to be seeing this kind of tree over and over again, we might as well start with it," Marion said. "This is your standard silver maple tree—it's the most common type of tree on the island and it's home to all sorts of critters, especially birds. I'll try to point out any notable birds if I see them, but usually they're a little shy when big groups come along."

Marion told them more about the tree, like how

long ago it had evolved into the tree it was today and how significant it was to Marigold's history. There was a time period over a hundred years before when a lot of the trees had been cut down to build homes, but with some effort, residents had saved the remaining ones from being cut down.

Once everyone got a good look at the trees, Marion led them to the next point of interest. She casually pointed out a few different plants of note, giving brief overviews before moving on. Eventually, they reached a small clearing with a bunch of green grasses and young trees, and Marion stopped them again.

She squatted down and plucked a few leaves of a plant from the ground.

"Does anyone know what this is?" Marion asked.

Grace looked at the leaves, cocking her head to the side. It looked like any other plant to her, but then again, that was why she was there. She hardly knew the names of flowers besides the simple ones like roses or daisies.

"It's sassafras," Joshua said with certainty.

"Exactly!" Marion's face lit up. "I think you're the first person in one of these groups to accurately recognize it without smelling it first. Here, let's pass it around. Sassafras is an edible plant that's a little rare around here, but you can find it in spades to the south of here. It was actually used in traditional root beer recipes to give it that flavor, and some people like to make their own sassafras syrups or teas at home."

She passed the plant to the person closest to her, who smelled it and nodded before passing it along.

"Wow, how did you know that?" Grace said quietly to Joshua as Marion told a story about finding a sassafras plant as a young girl.

"I'm a chef, and there was a trend toward wild edible plants a few years back. I never got into it since that's not quite my style, but I learned a little bit." Joshua shrugged.

"A chef? That's so cool!" Grace grinned. "What kind of food?"

"Mostly seafood and Italian. I own a restaurant in town." Joshua paused as the sassafras got passed to him. He sniffed it and handed it to Grace. Grace sniffed it and wrinkled her nose. "Not a fan?"

"I've never liked root beer. Like the very thought of it, even now, makes me want to shudder," she said, handing it off to the next person. "I think it's because it's kind of medicinal but kind of sweet, like someone dumped a bunch of simple syrup into medicine."

"So a spoonful of sugar doesn't help the medicine go down?"

"Definitely not," Grace replied with a laugh. "Anyway, I'd say I was jealous that you're a chef, but I think I'm more of a restaurant-goer than a restaurant owner."

"Oh yeah, it's a big difference." Joshua adjusted his hat as Marion led them to the next spot on their tour. "But that still doesn't stop me from enjoying food whenever I get the chance. I'll go way out of my way to enjoy the perfect version of something. There's a lot of good food on the island."

"I know. It's really cool, especially since it's such a small place. I haven't gotten the chance to try everything out, but the places my friends have taken me have been amazing." Grace practically salivated thinking about the Mexican-inspired lobster roll she'd had when she first got to the island. She wanted to go back to try it again.

"What have you tried? I haven't had the chance to go out to eat much lately," Joshua said.

"I loved that Mexican fusion restaurant on the edge of downtown, plus this little New York-style pizza spot where I had a slice a little while ago. But besides that, I've been indulging in a lot of desserts from Brooke's Bakery."

"I've heard about that spot. The pastries are supposed to be great." Joshua smiled. "And that pizza place is my go-to whenever I'm in that area. It tastes like the real deal, and it's easy to pick some up on the way home when I'm too tired to cook."

"I bet having to cook when you get home from a restaurant is exhausting."

"It can be. It's been a while since I've been in the kitchen for a full service, but I remember coming home from a busy night once and eating one of those little cups of macaroni and cheese that you put in the microwave."

"No!" Grace's eyes widened.

"Yeah. Actually, I'm pretty sure I did that *more* than once, since it was cheap. And there's something special about that fake cheese." Joshua's smile turned nostalgic. "My palate can be a little all over the place—I could eat those cups of macaroni and cheese and enjoy them, but I definitely appreciate a beautifully put together cheese plate too."

"A man of eclectic tastes." Grace laughed. "But I agree—sometimes you just want that unnatural orange stuff over a fancy, aged cheese."

"Exactly!"

Before Grace could tell him more about her mission to try as many foods from as many restaurants as she could, Marion stopped them again to show off a massive tree. Grace chuckled as Marion launched into another story about how she had climbed a smaller version of a tree just like this when she was a kid and fallen off, breaking her wrist. That didn't dampen any of her excitement about the plant itself, though.

Not much dampened Marion's excitement in general, even though every story she told seemed to end in her getting a bee sting, a scrape, or worse.

"It seems like a lot of these plants have a vendetta against her," Joshua said as they fell toward the back of the group.

"Or maybe she's just very forgiving." Grace shrugged. "Her enthusiasm is pretty contagious, though. Oh, look! It's another sassafras plant, right?"

Grace stopped and pointed out a plant that looked similar to what Grace had shown them, rubbing it between her fingers.

"You found more sassafras?" Marion said from the front of the pack. "Good eye!"

Grace mentally patted herself on the back. She had never had a green thumb or paid much attention to the specific plants she saw on her jogs or treks into nature for her photography, but now she wanted to.

"You don't want to grab some sassafras to take

home and throw into a dish?" Grace asked, sniffing the remnants of the sassafras on her fingers. It was a little more tolerable when she wasn't smelling it directly from the plant.

"Nope, not right now. I don't fully trust myself with these plants, as much as I trust Marion's knowledge." He tucked his hands into his pockets. "Plus, I've never been a root beer person either."

"Well, it's nice to know I'm not alone. It just tastes like medicine, like I said." Grace wrinkled her nose.

"Seriously."

"And here are some edible mushrooms!" Marion said with a thrilled gasp when they passed by a tree. "With mushrooms, you *really* have to be careful. Don't try to identify them off of pictures from a book when you're hunting for them, especially if you're unfamiliar with an area. You should only eat mushrooms that someone who's an experienced mushroom forager can vouch for. Poisonous mushrooms can literally be killer."

"And that's why I don't do much with wild edible plants," Joshua said to Grace, sliding into line behind other people who wanted to take a closer look at the mushrooms. "I've had a lot of chef friends have close calls with mushrooms especially."

"I never knew the life of a chef could be deadly."

"Neither did I, until my friends had their brushes with danger," Joshua said. "And there I was in my busy kitchen, worrying about burns. Oh, and whether anyone would somehow get sick even though I'm a bit neurotic about a clean kitchen."

"That's good to hear. I've seen a lot of those restaurant rescue shows where the kitchen and fridges are filthy." Grace shuddered. "It put me off going to restaurants for a while."

The group came to a clearing that extended all the way to the end of a bluff, the grass waist high.

"That's an aversion you seem to have gotten over. How long have you lived here?" Joshua asked.

"I grew up here, but we moved away when I was eighteen," Grace explained. "Then I was a caretaker for my father for a long time while he was sick, until he recently passed. Some of my friends who live here suggested that I come to Marigold to get a fresh start, so here I am."

"I'm sorry to hear about your father."

"Thank you." Grace ran her hand across the tops of the grasses that lined the trail. "It's been lovely revisiting the island again."

She had said the same thing to multiple people since her father's passing, but she truly felt it deep down with Joshua. Something about his gray eyes, partially shaded by the brim of his baseball hat, felt so sincere to her when he expressed his condolences.

Marion broke into another explanation of some prickly grasses that thankfully hadn't harmed her in the past, and they moved back into the woods again. She shushed everyone when she heard a bird and pointed it out before it flew off. Grace didn't spot it, but Joshua did.

As they walked to their next destination, Joshua entertained her with stories about the birds he'd had the most contact with—pigeons in the various cities he'd been to. He and pigeons were mortal enemies no matter where he went. Grace laughed so much that she knew all the birds in the area must have flown away from the noise she was making.

Over their brief lunch break, taken at a picnic area in a park, she told him stories about some of her favorite photo shoots. The conversation flowed easily, even between Marion's excited monologues about whatever plant or animal life they came across. Grace was learning so much that she would never be able to look at a field of grass on the island the same way again.

She hardly felt any soreness in her feet by the time they looped back around to the rec center, even though the class had lasted several hours. Time had completely flown by. The others in the group thanked Marion before peeling off to head to their respective cars. Joshua and Grace thanked her too, but they both lingered around the entrance of the center as if they didn't want to leave.

"Did you ever pick up your vase from the pottery class?" he asked.

"Nope, did you?"

"Nope. Want to go pick them up?"

"Sure, let's go," Grace said.

They chatted about their impressions of their nature class on their walk over to the pottery studio, where their works had been fired in a kiln and were waiting for them. Both of them agreed that they'd had a lot more fun than they anticipated, although Grace secretly thought her enjoyment was more because of Joshua's presence than because of the class itself—although Marion had been an informed and entertaining teacher.

When they arrived at the pottery studio, someone pointed them toward the back where the kiln and finished pieces were waiting.

"Wow, it's..." Joshua picked up his lopsided vase once he found it on the shelf of finished pieces.

"An even bigger masterpiece than you

remember?" Grace asked with a grin, picking up hers. It had come out slightly better than she'd thought it would.

"Exactly." He grinned too. "Yours turned out really well."

"You think so?" She turned it over in her hands a little. "I don't know where I'm going to put it in my room. It doesn't quite go with the aesthetic."

"I don't know where mine could fit either. Maybe we could trade?"

"Sure, why not? It'll be a fun souvenir." Grace handed her vase to Joshua and took his in return. "It'll look stunning on my dresser."

"This baby is going right in the middle of my mantle for everyone to see," Joshua said, a warm glint in his eyes.

"Please tell me that you'll say it's by an anonymous artist if anyone asks." Grace laughed.

"I promise," Joshua said. "Are there any other art classes in your future?"

"Like pottery? Not in the near future."

"What's your next class, then?"

"A dance class. How about you?" she asks, hoping his friend had somehow been on the exact same wavelength as she'd been when she'd signed up for classes.

"Now it's that dance class."

Joshua gave her another warm smile, which Grace returned. She couldn't wait to see him again. She just knew any class she took with him was going to be a lot of fun, just like today had been.

CHAPTER EIGHT

Lydia loved the way the late afternoon light cut into the office area of the inn, especially in the summer. She settled in the secondhand lounge chair that Angela had purchased and called her daughter Holly.

"Hey, Mom!" Holly said when she picked up. The sounds of Syracuse's campus came through in the background—music and excited laughter. "What's up?"

"Not much. I just wanted to see how things were going now that the semester is over."

"Really good! I can't believe I'm halfway done with my degree. I did well on my finals too."

"Wow, halfway done already?" Lydia could hardly believe it herself. It felt like she had been watching Holly painstakingly apply to multiple schools and tear open acceptance letters just weeks ago. "And congrats on your finals, sweetheart."

"Thanks! I'm still packing up a few things—I had to run and get some extra tape—but once I'm done I'm going to drive down to Boston to pick up Nicolas so we can come to Marigold."

Lydia smiled. "I'm so excited to see you both."

"We are too! I can't wait to get something to eat on the island," Holly said with a laugh. "I'm very, very tired of dorm food and so is Nicolas, though his options seem better. There's a lot more going on in Boston than up here."

Lydia hummed in acknowledgement. "Well, we'll definitely get some amazing food. And ice cream, of course, maybe with some brownies. And is this the first time you'll be seeing Nicolas since spring break?"

"Yup! I'm glad he transferred to a school in Boston, since it's way better than having a whole ocean between the two of us, but it's still a little hard." Holly sighed and the ruckus around her quieted. Lydia figured she had just gotten inside. "But we're still committed."

Lydia had to agree. They were young, but they were doing everything they could to stay together.

Transferring schools really showed her that Nicolas was invested in his relationship with her daughter. She was glad the young man would be staying more than a few days this time so she could get to know him better, especially if he and Holly were going to be in a long-term relationship.

"Well, I'll let you get back to packing. Text or call me once you're in Boston, okay?" Lydia asked.

"Will do. Love you, Mom."

"Love you too."

Lydia hung up and tucked her phone back into her pocket before heading out to the front desk. Kathy and Grace were looking at a fancy camera, chatting excitedly.

"Hey, Lydia," Grace said, looking up. "How's it going?"

"Good! What are you guys up to?"

"Just talking shop," Kathy said, twisting her red hair around her fingers and tugging it back from her face. "Grace is giving me so many amazing photography tips. I feel like I've just gotten my own private tutor."

"Oh, you're too nice." Grace chuckled. "It's been a while since I've really worked on it for more than just an afternoon since my dad was sick, but I made a bit of a living off selling pieces, so I have a little to share, at least."

"I'm ready to hear all of it." Kathy sounded excited, making Lydia smile.

Just as Lydia had noticed when she'd reconnected with Angela, it felt like Grace had slid back into her life just as seamlessly as she had when they were teenagers. Walking into the lobby and seeing Grace chatting with Angela or making someone laugh felt as natural as could be, as if she was meant to be there.

"I'd love to hear more about your photography, but I've got to head out to Angela's family's dinner," Lydia said, grabbing her purse from behind the front desk. "You two are totally welcome to come!"

* * *

The kitchen at Angela's parents' house had been renovated years ago, but on busy nights like this, it was always a little cramped. Angela and Brooke were putting together the last few dishes, occasionally bumping into one another or running out of counter space.

"Oops, coming up behind you two with a hot pan," Phoebe said to her daughters.

Angela and Brooke scooted to the side so that Phoebe could put a big casserole dish filled with vegetables down on a trivet.

"Wow, those look really good, Mom." Angela chewed her bottom lip, looking over the spread. "Are these all from your garden?"

"Yes, besides the carrots, which came from the farmers' market." Phoebe peeled off her oven mitts. "I hope the garden survives this little game of soccer or whatever they're doing out there."

Angela peeked out of the window above the sink into her parents' backyard, where Jake was kicking a soccer ball around with Travis and his girlfriend, Jennifer. Jake kicked the ball, and it sailed through the air, nearly hitting the little fence that Phoebe had set up around her plants. Her little boy took a tumble trying to chase after it and nearly fell into some tomatoes. All three women sighed, then laughed at how similar they sounded.

Family dinners were becoming more and more of a madhouse as time went on, but Angela wouldn't have traded them for the world. When she and Jake had moved back to Marigold, the dinners had gotten bigger and more consistent. Some weeks, the house was packed with friends and significant others.

This week was one of those ones. Travis and

Jennifer, plus Patrick, Hunter, Lydia, and Grant were there. Everyone fell into easy conversations, laughing and sipping on wine, or soaking in the slightly cooler weather of the evening outside.

Angela wasn't sure if Grace and Kathy were going to take Lydia up on her invitation, but there was more than enough food to go around if they showed up.

"Is this too salty for all of you?" Phoebe asked, holding up some zucchini. Brooke took a bite, then Angela did the same. "It's a recipe from one of my diet books. Well, if you can call throwing some zucchini and olive oil together before cooking it a recipe."

Ever since Phoebe had fainted last summer due to low blood pressure, she had taken care to make sure she had enough sodium in her diet. No one seemed to mind since Phoebe was a great cook—all of the "diet" foods she made were just a teeny bit different than what they would have made anyway.

Angela was glad the lifestyle transition had been a smooth one. Ultimately, Phoebe's health scare hadn't revealed any serious illness, but waiting at the hospital to see if her mother was okay wasn't something Angela wanted to experience again any time soon.

"I think it's fine," she said. "What else is in that cookbook?"

"Oh, the chicken is from there, as is that guacamole. Avocados have a lot of potassium, which I need too," Phoebe replied.

Brooke snagged a chip and dipped it into the guacamole. It didn't go with any of the other dishes they were having, but they had given up on thematically cohesive dinners a while ago and went with whatever everyone wanted. This week, there was honey mustard chicken, crispy roasted potatoes that were worth turning the oven on for in the summer heat, coconut milk rice, spicy baked beans, and an assortment of vegetables cooked in different kinds of ways.

"It's so good," Brooke said with a sigh.

"Hey, leave some for everyone else!" Angela admonished, snagging a chip too. "Especially Mom."

"You say that as you eat a bigger scoop than I do." Brooke nudged Angela with her hip, cocking an eyebrow.

"Well, it *is* super good." Angela held her hand up in front of her mouth to hide the food in it as she spoke.

"Oh, and speaking of things that are super good, I've modified a few treats from the bakery to be healthier," Brooke said, eating another chip plain. "Well, less indulgent."

"I like that—'less indulgent,'" Phoebe put in, cracking some fresh black pepper over the veggies. "It sounds a lot better than 'diet' this or 'low fat' that or whatever the trends are these days. Words like that always make whatever it is taste a little bit sadder."

"Yeah, that's how I'm going to pitch them to my customers—less indulgent, but still delicious. The muffins felt like a good place to start, since they're pretty popular around breakfast time." Brooke took the pepper from Phoebe and put it back on the shelf. "Is that ready to go to the table?"

"Yup, it is. And Angela, can you check on the rice?" Phoebe wiped her hands on her apron.

Angela nodded and tasted it, giving a thumbs up. "Perfect."

"All right, then. Let's get these in the serving dishes." Phoebe pulled some out and put them on the counter. "Anyway, what were you saying about the muffins?"

"I'm replacing some of the sugar with applesauce or mashed bananas, depending on the muffin. It's such an easy switch and it adds more nutrients without sacrificing sweetness," Brooke laid some chicken pieces into a big dish. "Like the banana nut muffin. A total no-brainer."

"I'll have to taste one of those," Angela said. "Eating a muffin every morning is good for the soul but probably not for my health."

"I'll bring some by the inn, then." Brooke dumped the sauce over the chicken. "Should we start calling everyone in to the table?"

"Yes, I think we're ready."

Angela was tasked with wrangling everyone inside and gathering them around the table. Her father, Mitch, helped bring the heavier dishes in before taking his seat at the head of the table next to Phoebe. They had purchased a bigger table recently, so there was enough room for everyone.

The commotion that had been all over the house was now concentrated in the dining room as everyone plated up their meals. Jake was great at eating his vegetables, especially when his grandmother made them, so Angela made sure to load up his plate with them, along with the chicken, which was his favorite.

Only the taste of so much delicious food could bring the noise level down several notches. Angela sighed in pleasure, scooping up the unlikely combination of coconut rice and the honey mustard chicken and eating it. It was addictive, and it seemed as though everyone else agreed.

"How's work been going for everyone?" Mitch asked, topping off Patrick's glass of wine.

"It's going well," Travis said. "Things are a little quiet now, but it's the calm before tourist season hits full force."

Angela nodded. Travis had been a Marigold cop for a while now, so she knew just how hectic his summers could be. The island was a very safe place to live, but there was always the risk of more petty crime with more people visiting.

"Same here," Jennifer said. "A lot of people have been buying homes, especially vacation homes. I'm leading so many showings that my head is spinning by the end of the day."

Everyone chuckled at that, as did Angela. Jennifer Lowry had fit right in with their family ever since the first time Travis had brought her to dinner. After months of pushing the two of them together, Angela was happy to see that she and Brooke had both had the right instincts when trying to set Jennifer and Travis up.

"And the bakery is going well, if those lines are to be believed," Travis said to Brooke with a smile. "I wanted to pop by to grab something for the office the other morning, but it looked like everyone else in Marigold beat me to it."

"Yeah, it's getting nuts! I'm going to have to hire more people soon." Brooke smiled, and Hunter squeezed her hand, pride clear in his eyes. Then she straightened a bit, an excited look passing over her face. "Oh, and Hunter has good news too."

"My movie finally has a release date in the winter," Hunter said. "I can't believe it. It feels like it's been in my head forever, and now everyone will get to see it."

"We'll all go see it together when it comes out," Angela promised him.

"You'll have to buy out half the theater to fit everyone in there," Patrick joked, making everyone else laugh too.

The meal continued on just like that, with easy conversation and good news all around. Mitch and Phoebe were keeping busy in their retirement and talked about going on a trip together soon. Jake was actually enjoying his summer reading list, especially with Patrick's help. The two of them would read in the living room together, keeping each other company. Lydia and Grant gave a few hints about their wedding plans, but Angela knew they hadn't hashed out all the details yet. They'd tell everyone everything when the time came.

After eating a full plate and finishing her glass of wine, Angela was content in a way that only family dinners could make her feel. Her limbs felt heavy and her stomach was perfectly full. She helped everyone clear the table once dinner was done, heading into the kitchen with Patrick behind her.

"If there's any leftover coconut rice, I'm going to inhale it," Patrick said, rinsing off Jake's plate.

"You might have to fight for it. It was a huge hit." Angela handed him the next plate for him to rinse.

"Two is better than one when it comes to leftover fights." Patrick grinned at her. "Maybe we could team up."

"Why do I get the feeling that you'll walk away with more of it than I do?" Angela laughed and nudged him with her elbow. "You've never left a leftover uneaten. Remember the pizza incident?"

Patrick had taken home a pizza from a restaurant a few weeks ago after a double date. Angela had made a detour to pick something up from Brooke and then headed over to Patrick's, only to find that he'd already eaten the leftovers only an hour after they'd finished the meal.

"That's true. But I'd always share with you." Patrick gave her a gentle kiss on the lips.

"Uh-oh, smooch alert," Brooke teased as she strolled into the kitchen, turning on the kettle for some tea to enjoy with dessert. "We've got a smooch alert, Travis. Lawbreakers, right in your midst."

"I know. I can't believe it," Travis said with a snort.

"You two will never stop teasing me, will you?" Angela asked, playfully glaring at both of them.

"Of course not. What else are siblings for?" Brooke asked, her blue eyes glittering.

Angela rolled her eyes and laughed. She would take their teasing any day as long as it meant she got to see them often. Being close to family was one of the best things to come out of her move to Marigold.

CHAPTER NINE

A few days after the big family dinner, Brooke's eyes opened before her alarm on her smartwatch vibrated to gently wake her up. Finally, she had gotten used to the incredibly early hours that running a bakery required. Peeling herself out of bed wasn't as big of a chore as it had once been.

She slid out of bed without waking Hunter, though that wasn't a difficult task. He was a deep sleeper and hardly stirred when she had a loud alarm going off. Still, she showered and moved around the bedroom stealthily in the dark as she got ready for work so she wouldn't wake him at all. He had been up late helping her out with some admin things for the bakery, and she knew he needed his rest.

Even though she had gotten a good feel for the

room after months of dressing in the near dark, she still opened Hunter's drawers sometimes. His was the second to the bottom, while Brooke's underwear drawer was one above it. She reached inside, and instead of feeling some lightweight socks, she felt something velvety.

She pulled the little object out and stared at it. It was a ring box. The temptation to open it was way too strong, so she did, her heart racing. The ring inside was absolutely gorgeous, and there was no mistaking what the ring was for. She stared at it for a few seconds. It was so brilliant that the diamonds caught in the low light coming in from a crack in the curtains.

She closed the box quickly and quietly, her heart pounding so hard that she thought Hunter would wake up and hear it.

Scratch meowed at her feet, nearly making her jump a foot into the air. She pressed a hand to her chest before scooping the kitten up as he purred. After giving him enough cuddles to stop him from meowing again, she put him on the bed next to Hunter. Hunter didn't wake up, but he rolled over toward Scratch, leaving just enough room for the cat to tuck himself against his chest. Hunter mumbled something in his sleep, but he didn't stir any more.

Brooke looked down at her boyfriend's sleeping form, her mind racing. Her heart hadn't slowed down either. Was it possible for someone's heart to explode? She felt like hers was about to do just that at any second.

She snapped out of it a few moments later and headed out to her car, dialing Angela's phone number as she did. Once she was inside her car, she hit the call button.

"Hello? Brooke? What's wrong?" Angela asked, her voice rough from sleep.

Her older sister kept early hours too, but Brooke was calling just a few minutes before Angela's alarm clock would probably have gone off. She felt a little bad, but this was serious. She needed to talk to someone, and it couldn't wait.

"Sorry to call at the literal crack of dawn, but I found an engagement ring in Hunter's sock drawer when I was getting dressed this morning," Brooke said in one breath.

"What?" Angela sounded completely awake now. "You're kidding!"

"Nope, I'm not." Brooke laughed, glad that she had left the house before calling. Angela's yelp was so loud that it *definitely* would have woken Hunter, even through the phone's speakers. "I'm literally still trembling."

"I would be too! What a way to wake up."

"I know, right? I doubt I'll need a cup of coffee. I'm that excited," Brooke said, pulling away from the house. "Okay, I doubt I'll need more than *one* cup. But I'm so thrilled. We've talked about it a little, and it feels so right."

"I'm so happy for you, Brooke."

"Thanks. Now I'm just freaking out about when it'll happen."

"Probably when you least expect it." Angela yawned and her alarm went off in the background. "Shoot. I've got to get going."

"Me too. Talk later."

"Sounds good. I definitely want to hear more about this. Love you!"

"You too."

Brooke hung up and finished her drive to the bakery. As she tied on her apron and started making her first batches of muffins for the day, she wondered when Hunter was going to pop the question.

And how would he do it?

* * *

Marigold was very easy to get around on foot, which Grace loved. She could really lose herself in these walks and relax, going wherever the paths led her. In the past few days, she had wandered into town, across a new park, and to a spot on the beach with a view she had never seen before. There were a lot of birds in the area, ones she could identify from her nature walk class. But today, she had a destination in mind.

She stepped onto a pier, checking the wooden railings until she found the one she was looking for. It was almost hidden amongst other people's carvings and was worn with time, but she found it—her name carved into the wood of the pier railing. Her father had taken her to this spot several times. She ran her hand over the carving, feeling the grooves in the wood.

She took a seat on the pier and looked out onto the water. The Grace who had carved her name into the wood was a very different person than the woman she was today. Both versions of herself had their strengths and weaknesses. Now that she had the chance to forge a new path, she wanted to take the best parts of both and take those attitudes forward.

Grace played with the zipper of her bag. She

hadn't brought her father's ashes with her today. Even though she knew she wanted to spread his ashes in the ocean and could've arranged to do it at any time, she wasn't quite ready to let go of that last little piece of him yet.

A few minutes later, her phone buzzed in her purse, letting her know it was time to head to her next class. Her mood lifted right away. Today was her dance class, and Joshua was going to be there. She hadn't danced in a long time, although she enjoyed it whenever she got the chance, despite her lack of formal training. She wondered if Joshua would be a good dancer, or if he could even stick to a beat.

She made it to the dance studio just as the handsome dark-haired man did. He was dressed in comfortable clothes the same way she was.

"Hey!" He greeted her with a warm smile. "Ready to bust a move?"

"Hopefully." Grace laughed. "I haven't danced in a long time, unless you count doing a little shoulder shimmy when I eat something delicious."

"I haven't danced in a long time either. Especially not in public."

"You don't dance when you taste something delicious?"

"Not at work, no." He chuckled. "But at home, all bets are off."

He opened the door to the rec center for her and let her walk inside ahead of him. They found the studio bustling with a few students who were in their late twenties to early forties, if Grace had to guess. She didn't feel like she was too young or too old for the class. She and Joshua found a spot toward the middle.

"Welcome to this intro to cha cha class!" a young woman said from the front. "I'm Alexis, and this is my dance partner Hans, and we'll be walking you through the basics that you can take anywhere. Are you guys ready to get started?"

Everyone nodded, and Hans clapped his hands together.

"Wonderful! Let's begin with a demonstration," he said.

Alexis turned on some upbeat music and they started dancing. Grace was instantly enthralled. They moved together in sync but maintained their own bit of flare to the dance. Hans twirled Alexis around with ease and supported her body so she wouldn't fall hard on the floor when he dipped her. Best of all, they looked like they were having a lot of fun. Once they finished, the entire class clapped.

"I've totally got that down," Joshua murmured to Grace as he clapped.

Grace laughed. "Do you, now?"

"I should clarify that I mean I've vaguely absorbed what I'm supposed to do and I'll probably end up looking like an octopus flopping around in shallow waters."

Grace stifled another laugh. Alexis and Hans let everyone introduce themselves and explain why they had signed up. Most people there came by themselves and just wanted to learn how to dance. A few others were there with a partner or friend and wanted to learn to dance at some upcoming events. Thankfully, no one had a lick of dancing experience besides some childhood ballet classes, putting Grace further at ease.

Then Alexis and Hans started their first demonstration. It was just three steps forward and three steps back, their hands joined between them.

"All right, got it?" Alexis asked. "Partner up and practice a bit."

"Want to be partners?" Grace asked Joshua.

"Yeah, definitely."

She took Joshua's hands, surprised at the flush in her cheeks when she did. His hands were very warm and felt a little rough, but the feel of his skin was pleasant against hers. Joshua started taking a few steps forward right as Grace did, so they nearly stepped on each other's toes. Both of them laughed.

"We're off to a great start, aren't we?" Grace said. "I'll go back and you can go forward."

She took three steps back as Joshua took three forward, then they switched. Joshua smiled when they got the hang of it.

"There we go," he said. "Now what?"

"You twirl me around and dip me five inches above the ground?"

"And then we go to the hospital when I accidentally drop you?" Joshua laughed this time. It was a big and warm laugh that Grace couldn't help but smile at.

"Okay, you guys are looking great!" Hans said. "Let's add to it."

Hans and Alexis demonstrated a more advanced move, then broke it down into smaller steps. It involved a little more touching than the last steps.

"We'll walk around and give tips as you all practice. Don't forget your posture," Alexis said, turning on some music.

"Okay. Sounds easy enough." Joshua turned to Grace and gently put one hand on her waist and took her hand. Tingles went down Grace's spine when he pulled her a little closer, and she looked down at her feet. She wasn't sure of her steps and definitely wasn't sure if she could look him in the eye without her cheeks going any redder.

Who am I, a fourteen year old girl at a school dance? Grace thought. Some things never changed.

After a bit of fumbling and laughing, they got the hang of it.

"Nice work, you two!" Hans called as he passed by them. "You're naturals."

"I don't know about that, but we're having fun," Grace said, finally looking at Joshua. His smiling gray eyes put her at ease again.

"Hey, that's all you really can do!" Hans laughed and moved on.

Once they got the basic steps down, they added a few more until they had a short routine down. Once everyone got a little practice, they took turns performing for everyone, three pairs at a time. Even though no one was perfect, Grace still felt a little bit of stage fright when it was her and Joshua's turn. But his reassuring nod before they started gave her a little boost of confidence.

"We did it!" Grace said as the class clapped for them.

"And no one's in the hospital with a broken bone," Joshua added.

Hans and Alexis told them about the dance party that they hosted two weekends a month and the intermediate class that they also offered if anyone was interested in learning more. They dismissed everyone after and people trickled out of the room. Thinking ahead for her upcoming classes, Grace asked for Joshua's number so they could touch base beforehand. He texted her so she would have his number too.

"Do you think you'll go for the intermediate class?" Grace asked as they walked out of the room slowly, lagging far behind the others.

"No idea. I might be pushing it with my dancing talents if I do." Joshua smiled and tucked his hands into his pockets.

Just like before, they lingered outside the front door of the building as if neither of them wanted to leave. Grace felt something in the air between them, an electric sort of energy she hadn't felt in a long time.

"I have to get to work," Joshua said, a note of disappointment in his voice. "But you should come by my restaurant tonight. Bring some friends, and I'd be happy to treat all of you. It's called Ariana."

"Really? That's so kind of you." Grace smiled, feeling a little surprised and honored that he'd do that for her. "I'll definitely take you up on that."

"Great. See you there." He gave her one more smile before he turned and walked toward his car.

CHAPTER TEN

"Hey, how was class?" Lydia asked Grace when her friend got back to the inn, rushing inside as though she was bursting with energy.

"You look like you had a good time," Angela added, leaning against the front desk.

Lydia had to agree—Grace was practically glowing, her skin colored with a healthy flush. Maybe it was the exercise doing good things to her, but Lydia had seen Grace come in from a long run a few days earlier, and she hadn't looked this happy then. She needed to know the full scoop.

"It was super fun!" Grace reported, beaming. "I managed to not break anything or anyone else's feet, so a little better than expected."

"Wait, what kind of dance class were you expecting?" Lydia asked with a laugh.

"I don't know, but I didn't want to push my luck. A good sense of rhythm doesn't mean much if I can't communicate that rhythm to my limbs, you know?" Grace adjusted her ponytail, which looked a little damp from sweat. "Oh, also, do you guys want to come out to dinner tonight? I heard about a great place. I know you guys will love it."

"Yeah, that sounds like fun!" Angela said.

"I'm in too!" Lydia was glad that both Grace and Angela were just as into food as she was. Now she had even more buddies to taste great dishes and try new restaurants with.

"Awesome. Let me take a shower and then we can go. I'll be ready in about forty-five minutes." Grace headed up to her room, and Lydia and Angela got back to work, wrapping up a few things that needed to be taken care of in the office.

Once Grace was showered and dressed, she reappeared downstairs, and the three women piled into her rental car to drive across the island. When they pulled up, Lydia realized that Grace had taken them to Ariana. The restaurant was busy, so Grace had to get a spot far away from the entrance.

Angela glanced over at Lydia as Grace parked the car, her eyes a little wide.

"How'd you find out about this place?" Angela asked as they got out of the rental.

"Oh, um..." Grace's cheeks flushed, and she did a terrible job of hiding it as she fumbled to put her keys back into her purse. "This guy I met in my classes owns it. We hit it off a bit, and he invited me to come with some friends for dinner."

"That's great!" Lydia said, grinning and bumping Angela with her shoulder when Grace turned to go inside the restaurant.

Angela exchanged an excited look with Lydia before glancing back at their friend. "This is totally wild. The guy's name is Joshua, right?"

"Yeah, it is." One of Grace's eyebrows went up. "Wait. Do you guys know him?"

"We do! He's great," Angela said.

"He's the guy we both wanted to set you up with!" Lydia said, excitement filling her. She had never been a big believer in fate, but her experiences on Marigold were starting to change that. "What are the odds?"

Grace's eyes widened, and she stopped walking. "Seriously?"

"Seriously."

"Wow, I had no idea." Grace blinked a few times, then continued on toward the restaurant, a slightly dazed look on her face. "What a coincidence."

* * *

Grace was still processing what she had just learned when they walked into the restaurant. Joshua was really the guy that they had thought would be a good match for her? The guy who they were super excited about because they knew they'd hit it off? She knew Marigold was a small island, but it felt *really* small in that moment.

Her heart fluttered as she looked around, taking in the restaurant. It was beautiful, light and airy with high ceilings and plenty of natural light, with a view of the ocean through the back window. Somehow, she felt Joshua's signature on it. It was a little upscale, but far from stuffy.

She swallowed, the flutter in her heart turning nervous. Was coming to dinner here a good idea? Was she looking too far into Joshua's invitation? Sure, they'd had a great time in their classes, and she definitely felt *something* when she was with him. But what did that even mean? And did Joshua feel like that toward her at all? She had no idea.

She hadn't come to Marigold looking for a relationship or anything, and it had been a long time since she'd been interested in dating, but now she found that she wasn't sure how she felt about the idea.

"Welcome to Ariana." The host greeted them with a smile. "Do you have a reservation?"

"We should. Joshua Marsden invited us," Grace said, clearing her throat and putting what she hoped was a confident and relaxed look on her face.

"Ah, of course! Follow me." The host gathered a few menus and a wine list before leading them through the busy restaurant.

Their table was right by the window and had the best view of the water.

"Wow, this is amazing! I didn't know this view was here," Angela said, scooting in.

"Me neither." Lydia looked around. "How cool is it that Joshua saved this table for us?"

"Really cool." Grace smiled, running her fingers along the leather outside of the menu.

She looked up and spotted the man himself coming out of the kitchen. He locked eyes with her right away and smiled, making Grace's cheeks flush with heat. He had showered and changed into nice dark slacks and a button-down shirt that was the same shade of gray as his eyes. She kept her composure—or at least she thought she did—and waved to him.

"Hey, guys!" Joshua said as he neared their table. He shook his head, looking surprised. "Grace, I didn't know you were friends with Angela and Lydia."

"Yeah, small island, right?" Grace said with a smile.

"I know!" Lydia laughed. "It's been a long time since we've seen you, Cap."

"Things are always a little nuts running a restaurant." Joshua rested his hand on the back of Grace's chair, and she felt hyper aware of his hand's warmth near her back. "Well, and the classes."

"Which ones have you taken?" Angela asked.

"All the ones Grace has—pottery, a nature walk, and the cha cha class. All of them were fun, but I don't know if we're going to start a pottery studio, survive off the land, or win a dance competition any time soon." Joshua laughed, as did the others.

"But hey, at least we tried." Grace shrugged, still smiling.

"True. I'm not sure if I would have had the guts to try the dance class if Grace hadn't been there," Joshua said.

"From the way both of you talk about it, this dance class sounded like some sort of obstacle course," Lydia commented with a chuckle.

"Sometimes it might as well have been." Grace glanced up at Joshua. "An obstacle course where we had to avoid stepping on each other's toes. If we were being graded, we probably would have gotten a B+ on that part."

"Oof, a B+? I'd say at least an A-." Joshua checked his watch. "Shoot. Sorry, I've got to get back there again. But I'll have our head chef Alan send out all of our favorites and some wine too, if you don't mind."

"That sounds great," Grace said, and the others agreed.

"Perfect." Joshua gave them one last smile, his eyes lingering on Grace for an extra moment before he headed off to the kitchen.

"I'm so excited!" Angela said. "I've heard so many good things about this place, and Cap always makes me drool when he talks about it. I can't believe we didn't come sooner."

"I know, right? But I'm glad we came today. We wouldn't have gotten the star treatment without Grace here." Lydia waggled her eyebrows. "Good thing she worked her charm."

"Oh, I don't know." Grace pressed her hands subtly to her face, trying to cool her flaming cheeks. "I don't think I've worked much charm."

Before Angela or Lydia could say otherwise, a waiter arrived with a few small carafes of white wine for each of them, almost like a wine flight.

"Hello, ladies," the waiter said with a smile. "We have a little sampling of our favorite house whites for you to try. Let us know which one you love the most and we can send out a bottle with your meal. These have been hand-selected to go with your meal tonight."

The waiter explained what each wine was and what its flavor profile was like. Grace nodded along. She knew a tiny bit about wine, but all of this was a little over her head. She smiled to herself—taking a wine class with Joshua would probably be like bringing a professional skier on a bunny hill.

"Wow, thank you," she said when the waiter finished up the explanations.

"Enjoy."

Grace took a sip of the wine she gravitated to first, which had a mineral flavor that she hadn't had before. It was delicious, and so were the others. The first one won out.

"I love this one." Grace pointed to the wine she liked.

"Same. It's so good." Angela drained the last of hers.

"I'm glad we're all in agreement." Lydia drained her small carafe too. "Let's go with this one for the meal."

They didn't have to wait long for the waiter to come back with the appetizer course. Grace's eyes widened when she saw the selection that Joshua had requested for them.

"Here we have arugula, prosciutto and pesto bruschetta, caprese salad, stuffed mussels," the waiter said, gesturing to each one. "The stuffed mussels are my personal favorite and I'm not even a mussels type of gal."

Once the waiter left, they all went for the mussels. When her first bite hit her tongue, Grace had to close her eyes. She could take or leave mussels most of the time, but these were incredible. The flavors burst over her tongue, so many that it took her a few moments to pinpoint each one. Next she tried the bruschetta, which tasted fresh and herby, but somehow didn't feel heavy like bruschetta she'd had at other restaurants had tasted. She rounded it out with the caprese salad. The tomatoes tasted like they had been picked moments before they made the salad.

The three of them were so focused on the appetizers that they didn't even see Joshua coming until he was right at their table.

"Silence all around," Joshua said, grinning. "I hope that means you're enjoying everything."

"It's insanely good. Especially with the wine," Angela told him, putting her hand to her chest. She shook her head, making her blonde hair sweep over her shoulders. "You're going to have a hard time getting us to leave if the rest of the food is this good."

"I'm glad to hear it. And you're going to love the main course." He looked at Grace, his smile turning more personal, like he had a secret only she could know. "I debated putting some wild edible plants into one of the daily specials, but I didn't want to press our luck."

Grace snorted. "Yeah. It probably would have gotten its revenge on us like all of those plants that attacked Marion."

Both Angela and Lydia looked confused, so Grace told them all about Marion and her enthusiasm for plants, despite the fact that her love of nature often seemed to lead to her getting injured in some way. She laughed along with everyone else, warmth filling her chest. She wasn't sure if it was the food or the company or both.

A little while later, Joshua slipped away to check in on some other customers, and the ladies enjoyed the final remnants of their appetizers.

"It's nice of him to keep stopping by our table like that," Lydia said, shooting Grace a look.

Grace shot her one back, raising an eyebrow. Was Lydia implying that he was checking on them because she was there? "He's a good business owner. I can tell he really cares."

"Yeah, he's super passionate about everything around his business," Angela said, seemingly oblivious to the look Lydia was giving Grace because she was busy pouring herself more wine. "I totally get that. It's like us and the inn."

Their conversation drifted to what was going on at the inn until the main course arrived. It was served family style—a big bowl of seafood arrabbiata, poached fish in a delicate broth, and fregula ai frutti di mare, the latter of which Grace had never heard of before. It looked almost like couscous, though it was made out of pasta dough, and was filled with fresh seafood.

Joshua and his chefs had outdone themselves. Everything was just as delicious as the first course.

The pasta was flavorful ,with a kick of spice that Grace adored, and the fish was so light and flaky that it melted in her mouth.

"I'm tempted to pick up that fish dish and chug that broth," Lydia said with a longing sigh.

"Same here." Grace took an extra spoonful and tipped it into her mouth. It tasted like the ocean without being fishy or overpowering.

"I know we're Joshua's guests and all, but I feel like doing that would get us kicked out," Angela said with a chuckle.

"Who knows—maybe we can push the limits." Grace laughed, the effects of the wine and the warmth of the food making her feel looser than she had in a while.

They polished off all the food except for one little piece of pasta.

"So good, right?" the waiter asked when she picked up their empty dishes.

"It's all been incredible," Grace said. "Thank you."

"I hope you all saved some room for dessert." The waiter gave them a grin. "But it's always easy to make room for dessert, right?"

"Totally." Lydia laughed, her green eyes twinkling.

The waiter cleared their table and another member of the waitstaff came to sweep stray bits of food off the tablecloth. Grace sat back in her seat. She was full, but the waiter had been right—she could always make room for dessert.

"You guys look like you're having an awful time," Joshua joked when he reappeared.

"Everything has been so, so delicious," Grace gushed. She couldn't even make a joke about anything being bad here.

"Good. I have a special place in my heart for all of those recipes." He rested his hand on the back of Grace's chair again. She was feeling a little tipsy, so she didn't feel hyper aware of his hand this time around. It felt good. Almost... *natural* to have him so close to her. "Which one was your favorite?"

"The fregola," Grace replied readily. "I hadn't even heard of that before and it blew my mind."

"Same here," Lydia and Angela said without hesitation.

"It looks like we all agree." Joshua beamed with pride. "I learned how to make it when I was on a trip to Italy, and knew that I had to put it on my menu."

He took a little step back when the waiter arrived with all of their desserts. Grace found her appetite again the moment she laid eyes on everything.

"Here we have some goat milk and blackberry panna cotta, a lemon semifreddo, and of course, tiramisu," Joshua said. "Do you guys need anything else? Coffee, maybe?"

"Coffee would be lovely," Angela said.

"Great." Joshua nodded to the waiter, who nodded back and headed toward the kitchen. "I'll get out of your hair. Enjoy, you guys."

They all thanked him, and Grace watched him walk away for a moment.

"I think he likes you," Angela said.

"What?" Grace pulled her attention from Joshua. "You think so?"

"Yeah, one hundred percent." Lydia took one of the mini panna cottas onto her plate, right as the coffee arrived. "He looks at you with that vibe."

"Huh. Interesting." Grace tried not to smile, but she couldn't help herself. "I think you guys might be right, maybe."

The table fell silent as they tried the desserts. By that point, Grace thought it was impossible for the food to be any better, but the dessert proved her wrong. Everything had flavor, not just sweetness, and didn't feel like it would weigh her down after.

"You should ask him to go with you to Patrick's book signing next weekend," Angela told her. "It's going to be a lot of fun."

Grace sipped her coffee, considering it. Another little flutter went through her belly, although her stomach was too full for the butterflies to really get going. "You know what? I think I will."

"Yes, go for it!" Lydia encouraged, nodding enthusiastically.

They chatted a little bit until Joshua came back to check on them. After complimenting him on the deliciousness of all the food, Grace steeled herself, digging deep to find her courage.

"Would you like to come to Patrick Devlin's book signing next weekend?" she asked the tall, dark-haired man.

"Ah, I wish I could, but I can't." He grimaced. "I'll be out of town doing things for the new restaurant I'm hoping to open."

Grace could practically feel Lydia and Angela's disappointment coming off them in waves, but she kept her chin up. Her visit to Marigold was already great and she didn't come looking for love anyway.

"No worries," she said, letting go of her disappointment as she found a smile. "Good luck with your meetings."

"Thanks." He grinned down at her, although regret seemed to shine in his eyes. "Business calls again. I'll see you all later?"

"Yeah, of course. Thanks so much for an amazing night," Grace said.

Angela and Lydia echoed their appreciation, and Joshua beamed at them.

"It was my pleasure."

CHAPTER ELEVEN

Joshua frowned at his laptop, taking a sip from the mug of coffee he'd just refilled. What had he been working on? He'd gotten up to get himself a fresh cup of coffee and then forgotten what he'd been doing. It was right on the tip of his brain, but just far away enough for him to not easily recall it.

He clicked on his email and suddenly remembered. He'd been in the middle of returning a message about some work for the potential new restaurant. His trip to Boston was coming up soon, so he had to follow up on a few things in preparation.

Even though he had taken care of his immediate problem of losing his train of thought, he was annoyed at his lack of focus. He couldn't remember the last time he'd felt this scattered. This morning, he had nearly walked into the bathroom to take a shower with the burner still on in the kitchen, an empty pan set on top. He hadn't realized he'd put his shirt on backwards until he'd gotten to the restaurant, where he'd slipped into the office to turn it around. He'd poured salt into his coffee instead of sugar *twice* before he'd gotten it right.

Joshua sighed.

Maybe Alan was right—surviving on coffee and a few hours of sleep, grinding himself to the bone wasn't the recipe for success that it had been when he was younger. His body couldn't take that kind of stress. He sighed again and ran a hand through his hair. Maybe he needed to change things up and adjust his lifestyle to focus on a little more than just work.

He dove into his to-do list for the day, but his mind was still split between his email and Grace. There was nothing like the pleasure he got from feeding people a delicious meal with a good glass of wine, especially when he could make a woman like her light up the way she had after every bite.

He had attended to his other guests and checked in with his cooking staff, yes, but he'd always had an eye on her table. She really did dance a little when she tasted something delicious—just a little wiggle in her chair, like she couldn't help herself. It was incredibly endearing,

"You all right in there?" Alan asked, knocking on the office door. His chef whites were unbuttoned over a black t-shirt.

"What?" Joshua looked up sharply, his eyes going wide. Then he let out a breath. "You scared me."

"Wow, you must really be distracted." Alan walked in farther and sat down at the extra seat Joshua had put next to his desk for just this reason.

Joshua laughed and ran his hand over his face. "I guess I am. I'm just thinking about this woman I met in those classes. She was the ticket the other night that got the works and that new white wine we got in from California. Her and her friends, I mean."

Alan paused for a moment, then nodded. "I remember that. You really pulled out all the stops for them. And wow, that's great. I don't think I've ever seen you distracted by a woman before."

"It is pretty great." Joshua sat back in his seat and folded his hands over his stomach. "She's a lot of fun. Those classes you signed me up for aren't so bad when she's in them. Even the dancing and the pottery, which aren't my strong suits by a mile."

"I know, and that's exactly why they were a perfect choice." Alan broke into a grin, waggling his eyebrows a bit. He was a few years younger than Joshua, with a thin face and smile lines around his mouth.

"You're a little evil, you know that?"

"Evil? Me?" Alan put on a face that was the picture of innocence, looking around as if asking the walls to back him up. Then he gave up the act, chuckling. "But jokes aside, that's great, man. I can't believe you actually took my advice and got out there. I didn't think you'd last past one class, much less three."

"Yeah, yeah." Joshua had to smile too. "I can admit when I'm wrong. Sometimes."

"So what are you going to do about this woman in your classes? What's her name?" Alan asked.

"Her name is Grace," Joshua said. "And I don't know yet. She asked me to go to a book signing next weekend."

"Like a date?"

Joshua shrugged. "Dunno. But that's the weekend I'm going to Boston anyway, so I turned her down, as much as I want to go."

Alan raised his eyebrow at Joshua. "Josh. That weekend is pretty arbitrary, right? You can move things around since you're the boss of this whole situation?"

"Yeah."

"So you can take one night off. Nothing will explode." Alan shrugged, running a hand over his sandy blond hair. "We're a pretty well-oiled machine, if I say so myself."

"I know. But you're sure you'll be fine?"

"I'm totally sure. When was the last time you had to be hands-on in the kitchen because someone couldn't cut it?" Alan asked. Joshua didn't have an answer. "Exactly."

Joshua paused, taking a deep breath. "You're right. I'll call her and tell her I'll go."

"Good luck." His friend stood and clapped Joshua on the shoulder before leaving him to make the call.

Joshua grabbed his phone and found Grace's number. He was grateful that they had exchanged contact info on their way out of the dance class, or he wouldn't have had an easy way to reach her. He swallowed, then hit send before he could find a reason not to.

Grace answered after a couple rings. "Hello?"

"Hey, Grace. It's Joshua," he said.

"Yeah, hi! What's up?" She sounded upbeat, as if she had gotten a good night's rest.

"I just wanted to see if that invite to the book signing is still available. I had a change in my plans, and I'd love to go with you."

"Really? That would be great!" she said.

She told him the details of when it would take place and they set up some plans for the night. By the time the call was over, Joshua couldn't wipe the smile off his face. He said goodbye and hung up, his chest filling with a warmth that was a blend of excitement, happiness, and nerves.

He was aware he was an attractive guy—it would have been silly to pretend he wasn't. Patrons hit on him all the time at the restaurant, and he had perfected his polite rejections. He had never made time in his life for relationships, especially once he'd started his career as a restaurateur. The last serious girlfriend he'd been in a relationship with had probably been when he was twenty or so, and they hadn't dated for very long.

He put his phone face down on his desk, feeling a surge of focus again, and sent out an email to postpone his trip to Boston. After he hit send, tension melted from his shoulders. It was strange, but it felt good to put something ahead of work for once.

***

"And here are your keys," Angela said to the couple that she had just checked into the inn. "Let me show you both to your room."

She headed up the stairs, making small talk with the couple as she did. Everything with their guests had been going smoothly lately, and the flow of their bookings was pretty steady. Things had been a little bit bumpy at the start, with impatient guests who couldn't be pleased and hiccups in the day to day systems that they had now perfected. Nowadays, Angela was much more confident in her ability to bounce back from any hurdle that was thrown at them.

Once she made sure the guests had everything they needed and told them that someone would be at the front desk if they had any additional questions or requests, she headed back downstairs. The door opened again as she stepped behind the desk, and a bunch of flowers appeared before a delivery man did —the bouquet was that big.

"Hey there," the delivery man said around the flowers. "I have a delivery for Angela Collins?"

"Oh. That's me."

"Perfect." The delivery man put the vase of

flowers down on the front desk. "If you could sign here, that would be great."

Angela signed and thanked him, searching for the card attached. There were so many flowers, a gorgeous blend of greenery and fresh blooms, that it was a little hard to find. Eventually, she found the car tucked under a ribbon around the vase, and pulled it out to open it.

Happy eight month anniversary, Angela. Well, eight months since we made things official. I'm so glad we found each other when we did.

Love, Patrick

Angela smiled and pressed the note to her chest. She hadn't been expecting this at all—she knew it was eight months since they'd made it official, but hadn't thought much of it. Patrick was so busy with his book release coming up soon, but he had still taken the time to do something this sweet for her. Her heart fluttered just like it had when they'd first admitted their feelings for each other.

She took the flowers to the back office so that they would be out of the way, humming a happy song as she did. The flowers were yet another reason why she knew things were different with Patrick. Scott had never done anything like this for her in all the time they had been together, not even early on.

At most, he remembered their wedding anniversary if Angela initiated the plans for it, and he always got her flowers that he'd clearly picked up in haste from the grocery store. It was like his mind had always been elsewhere—which had probably been the case.

She never had to guess where she and Patrick stood. No matter how busy he was or how stressed he was, he always gave Angela one hundred percent of his attention when they were together.

Once she put the flowers down, she called Patrick.

"Hey, I just wanted to tell you that I got the flowers," she said when he answered, still smiling. "Thank you. They're gorgeous."

"Of course." There was a smile in his voice too. "I'm glad they got there. I thought I had missed the cut-off date for the delivery since there's so much going on. Sorry it was last minute."

"Oh my gosh, don't apologize at all! They're so thoughtful and beautiful. Even if you had sent them a day later I wouldn't have minded." Angela sniffed the flowers again. "You're neck deep in stuff for your book. How are things going?"

"Not bad. It's just a whole avalanche of emails and social media and all that. I get that tweeting or posting on Instagram is good for marketing, but sometimes I wish we could go back to when promoting a book was a little simpler." He chuckled. "Does that make me sound like an old man?"

"A tiny bit, but it's understandable. It's endearing."

"Now I feel young again." Patrick full-on laughed. "I love you."

"I love you too." Angela glanced at the clock, biting her lip. She had to leave soon. "I've got to go, though. I just wanted to let you know I got the flowers and that I adore them so much. See you later."

"Looking forward to it. Bye."

She hung up and headed back to the front desk, finding that Kathy had already taken her place. With the front desk taken care of, she went to gather Jake and all of his bags. He had packed them earlier with her help, excitedly talking about all the fun things he was going to do with Scott in Philadelphia.

"Ready to head to the airport to meet Daddy, honey?" Angela asked.

"Yup!"

She felt a tug of sadness in her chest at the thought of being away from her son again. He was going to spend a chunk of his summer with Scott, which she knew was good for him, but she was sure it would always feel difficult to say goodbye to her little boy. Scott was going to meet them at the airport and fly back to Philly with Jake.

Angela buckled Jake into the car and hopped into the front seat, pulling out of her parking spot. As much as she wanted to delay the inevitable, she couldn't draw out the drive over to the airport, since they were barely on schedule as it was.

"How old do I have to be to read Patrick's new book?" Jake asked out of the blue.

"Much, much older." Angela chuckled and looked at him in the rearview mirror. "Why?"

"Just want to." Jake shrugged. "Patrick is so cool."

"He is." She grinned, returning her gaze to the road.

To say Jake adored Patrick was a bit of an understatement at this point. The two of them got along incredibly well, with Patrick acting as a positive role model for the little boy. Jake's grades in English class had gone way up, and he was dragging Angela to the library for him to pick out new books every week. Patrick always took the time to help him with homework and was always happy to kick around the soccer ball with him when Angela was worn out.

She had to smile to herself. Patrick was really

even better than she could've ever dreamed he would be.

"Are you guys gonna get married?" Jake asked.

"We aren't in a hurry to, but I care about him a lot. " She laughed a little. There was nothing like the straightforward way kids asked questions. "He's going to be in our lives for a long, long time."

"Good." Jake looked out the window, a smile still on his face.

Angela's smile didn't waver either.

CHAPTER TWELVE

Grace studied herself in the mirror for a few moments, pleased with what she saw.

She usually threw her hair into a ponytail most days because it was practical, but today, it was down and blow-dried into submission around her shoulders. The floral-printed dress that she had bought almost impulsively when she'd gone shopping for her trip still fit just as nicely as it had in the dressing room too. It hugged her body and flared out around her knees, held up by spaghetti straps.

It was a little bit more daring than what she usually wore, but she wasn't uncomfortable in it. She touched up her makeup a little, gave herself another once over, and smiled. Even though her dress was earth-toned with a subtle green and white botanical print all over, shades that she thought would make her look dull at first, she couldn't help but notice the brightness in her eyes. The drab woman she had seen in the mirror when she'd first come to the island was gone.

She figured part of it was the makeup, all the sleep she was getting, the delicious food she was eating, and the scenery. Any of those things would have perked up someone's appearance on their own. But she knew another part was coming from inside of her, an inner satisfaction and contentment that she hadn't felt in ages. She felt lighter, more alive.

Her phone buzzed on her dresser, making her heart flutter. It was a text from Joshua, letting her know he was downstairs. He had come to pick her up, like it was a real date.

She gave herself one more look in the mirror, smiling at the thought of seeing Joshua again, before sliding on her sandals and heading down. He was waiting in the lobby, looking at some of the art that was up on the walls.

"Hey," she said, almost shyly.

"Hi." He looked at her and smiled broadly. "You look great."

"Thanks. You do too." And he did. He was wearing dark blue pants and a lightweight white linen button-down. It was a simple outfit, but he wore it well. His dark hair was swept off his forehead, but still a little bit messy like it always was. She liked it that way. He wasn't too stuffy about his appearance, but he still cared enough to dress nicely when the situation called for it.

They hopped in his car and headed to Bayside Books, the adorable bookstore that was hosting Patrick's book signing. It looked smaller on the outside than it was on the inside, and had the same white wood siding as many of the shops in town. The bright, sunshine-colored sign stood out against the building and the other business around. There was a huge banner in the window with the book's cover next to Patrick's headshot, proudly declaring that he was a local author.

"Wow, quite the turnout," Joshua said as they stepped into the shop. There wasn't much space to stand with the seats the event organizers had put out.

"I know! I'm glad we got here when we did." Grace looked around and spotted Angela and Patrick talking to someone who must have been an employee of the store. Grace waved, and they both waved back. "Hopefully we'll get a chance to actually talk to Patrick. He'll probably get swarmed after."

"I bet. I don't know him all that well, but I knew

his work was popular. This really drives home just how well-loved his books are." Joshua looked around. "He's probably having a signing in Boston too, right?"

"I think so. I don't see why he wouldn't, since it's so close." Grace ran her fingers along a shelf of half-priced paperbacks. "So everyone here must be locals, then."

"That's great."

Since it was so busy, Grace and Joshua went ahead and sat down before long, finding some seats with a good view of the podium before they got taken. Soon, the woman that Patrick and Angela had been talking to stepped up to the podium and tapped on the microphone, quieting the crowd.

"Thanks so much for coming out tonight," the woman said, her excitement clear in her eyes even from where Grace was sitting. "We're so excited to have a local author here tonight with his latest book. You all know him, and so do people across the globe—please welcome Patrick Devlin to the podium."

Everyone clapped and cheered as Patrick stepped up, a shy smile on his face and his book under his arm. He was wearing a dark blue blazer and a white shirt, both of which were pressed neatly. His brown hair was a little messy though, as if he'd nervously run his hands through it.

"Thanks so much for coming, everyone," Patrick said. "I've never seen this little shop so full and I've been coming here for years."

He put his book on the podium and, as Grace had suspected, ran his hands through his hair absently.

"I'm never sure where to start when I talk at signings. I've been working on this book for months and months, trying to keep it all under wraps, and now that I can actually talk about it, I'm at a loss for words." He chuckled and went to run his hand through his hair again, but stopped. He chuckled. "If I keep messing with my hair, I'm probably going to be bald by the end of this."

Everyone laughed, and some of the tension eased out of Patrick's shoulders.

"Anyway, I think the easiest place to start would be at the beginning of my writing process. It feels like all of my books come together in a different way," he said. "I got the first spark of inspiration for this when I was walking around the paths near where I used to live one damp fall evening. And that one spark turned into this whole book. That makes it sound simple, though. If you ask my girlfriend, Angela, she'd agree that it was anything but simple."

A few chuckles went through the crowd as

Patrick looked toward where Angela was sitting. The love he had for her was so clear, even in just a glance. It melted Grace's heart.

"Usually, my biggest problem is writer's block. To use writer lingo, I'm somewhere between a plotter—someone who outlines their books—and a pantser, or someone who just writes and sees where things go. So sometimes I make a right turn and realize that I've written myself into a corner."

He gave an almost theatrical grimace at that, and the crowd laughed.

"Most of the time," he continued, "my solution to that is a walk. It's good for my health and all. But then I end up walking to the Sweet Creamery or Brooke's Bakery, so I negate any health benefits I got from that walk."

"Hey, desserts are good for the soul!" Brooke chimed in from somewhere in the front of the audience, just loudly enough for Grace to hear. Both Grace and Joshua snorted. "And I'm not just saying that because I have skin in the game."

Patrick chuckled, resting his hands on the side of the podium. "I have to admit that the combination of one of your peanut butter blondies plus some chocolate fudge ice cream got me through several blocks, including one I had while writing the chapter that I wanted to read for all of you today. It's toward the beginning, so there aren't any spoilers. I wouldn't do that to you guys."

He read an excerpt of the book, a scene that was well-written and engaging, drawing Grace in immediately. The room was quiet as a pin until he closed the book, then everyone erupted into applause. Once the clapping died down, Patrick answered some questions before the woman who had introduced him gave everyone instructions for the signing.

Grace and Joshua each bought a copy and had their books signed before efficiently being swept to the adjacent outdoor area where there would be a small reception for those who wanted to stay. She saw a number of people she knew, including Lydia's aunt Millie, plus a lot of Angela's and Lydia's friends. Grace and Joshua got plastic cups of wine and clinked them together before taking a sip.

"Patrick did a great job up there," she said. "I'd probably collapse from nerves if I had to look up and see everyone's faces as I read from my book."

"Yeah. When I first got out of culinary school, I would try to watch people tasting my food to see what their reactions were. It didn't go well."

"Oh no! Why?" Grace couldn't imagine anyone disliking Joshua's food.

"Oh, they liked the food, but it still got me too in my head. I eventually decided I had to stay back in the kitchen." He chuckled. "I only did it once or twice, when there was a special I was particularly proud of."

The whole outdoor area erupted in applause again when Patrick came out several minutes later, his fingers linked with Angela's. Grace and Joshua waited for him to get his wine and his bearings before approaching him.

"Hey, congrats!" Grace said when they finally got to him, giving him a hug. She'd seen him around the inn a lot since she'd arrived a few weeks ago, and she had liked him immediately.

"Yeah, congrats," Joshua added, shaking Patrick's hand.

"Thanks!" Patrick smiled. He looked relieved now that the public speaking part of the night was over, or at least, that's what Grace assumed to be the reason. "I'm glad you guys could make it."

"We wouldn't miss it. I don't get to have famous authors sign my books, well, *ever*, really." Grace chuckled. "I'm so excited to binge-read the whole book tonight."

Before Patrick could say anything else, someone he recognized caught his attention and said hello. Grace and Joshua said their goodbyes and let the other person get a moment of Patrick's time.

They didn't have to wait long to get swept into another conversation. One of Joshua's frequent customers spotted him and came over to chat for a while about his family and the fishing trip they'd gone on. Grace smiled. Joshua's customers seemed to love the man just as much as they loved his restaurant. After a pleasant chat, Joshua slipped away to the bathroom and Grace spotted Lydia talking with a few women she didn't recognize.

"Hey, Lydia!" Grace said, gently putting her hand on her friend's shoulder.

"Grace, hi! I'm so glad you came over here." Lydia gestured Grace closer. "I wanted to introduce you to some other small business owners on the island—this is Leah, who runs a hair salon, Cora, who co-owns that neat little butcher shop with her husband, and Nicole, who runs the art gallery that we collaborate with from time to time. A lot of the pieces in the inn are from her gallery."

"So nice to meet you!" Grace said, shaking all of their hands. "How did all of you meet?"

"Millie hosts a small business owners group and

connected us all together," Lydia told her. "These ladies were seriously lifesavers when Angela and I were just starting the inn, and they still come to our rescue sometimes."

"Hey, now you're the one saving us from time to time," Leah interjected with a grin. She appeared to be the youngest member of the group. If Grace had to guess, she'd peg her to be in her twenties. "That marketing advice you gave me has seriously helped."

"I'm glad to hear it!" Lydia beamed. "I was feeling like an information leech for a while there."

"Oh, don't!" Cora laughed, a big smile putting dimples in her cheeks. "The group is far from one-sided."

"And speaking of groups, I was thinking about starting a book club," Nicole said, drumming her fingers on the side of her book. "I was just saying that it's been a long time since I've read consistently, and with the success of our business group, a separate book club sounded like a fun thing to do."

"I love that idea! I've been wanting to read more too," Leah said. "It's been on my New Years' resolution list for the past five years, and I haven't made much headway."

"Let's do it, then!" Lydia turned to Grace. "Are you in?"

"I'd love to join." Grace nodded enthusiastically, looking at the group of women around her. "For as long as I'm in town, anyway, you can count me in."

Reconnecting with Lydia and Angela had brought her so much happiness, and the thought of making more new friends for the first time in a long time sounded like a great way to step out of her comfort zone, just as she did in all of her classes. Having been so focused on caring for her father for years had made her forget just how many different people she got along with.

The voice in the back of Grace's head pinged back to a conversation she'd had with Angela and Lydia the other day. Both of them had mentioned plans in the far off future, like little day trips to nearby towns or visiting new restaurants when they opened, wishing Grace would stay on the island more permanently. Grace was tempted to. After all, she had no obligations elsewhere and her career wasn't tied to any particular location. Photographers could find work wherever there were people wanting their special moments captured.

Joshua came into view over Cora's shoulder, clapping his hand on Grant's shoulder and laughing at something the gruff-looking man said.

Grace sighed.

In the short time she had been on the island, she had gotten used to seeing the handsome restaurateur from time to time. That wasn't something she wanted to give up, at least not yet.

Now she was even more tempted to stick around.

* * *

Joshua hadn't had this much fun in a while. Grace was amazing company, of course, but he was having a great time talking to Grant and Patrick, too. The latter man had finally gotten a little more chance to breathe after the initial rush of fans came to thank him. The three of them had more in common than Joshua had thought, despite their three very different career paths.

Joshua glanced over toward Grace from time to time, watching her laugh with a few friends while keeping one ear attuned to the conversation going on around him. She seemed so relaxed and in her element talking with everyone.

"It's just business as usual," Grant said to Patrick. "Covered in mulch, bugs everywhere…"

Business.

Joshua blinked. It had been a while since he'd thought about his business, which was unusual.

Generally, it was on his mind more often than not. His to-do list seemed to have a permanent spot in his subconscious, constantly being added to. Even eating a meal or sipping some wine brought up thoughts about his menu or some future specials most times, but not now.

Joshua sipped his wine, nodding along as Grant continued his funny story about a recent landscaping project. Grant's business was successful, but he clearly spent a lot of time doing other things. He had his relationship with Lydia, his friendships with everyone at the inn, and a few hobbies beyond landscaping—all things that Joshua had always assumed were too time intensive for a business owner to keep up. It made him reconsider his carefully laid plans.

He had worked hard all his life, throwing himself into culinary school, the jobs in kitchens he'd gotten afterward, and finally into his business. Being a chef was far more stressful and competitive than most people knew. He'd spent hours upon hours on his feet, working from the bottom of the pile where he diced hundreds and hundreds of vegetables without getting a chance to actually *cook* anything.

As he'd climbed through the ranks, his drive had only gotten stronger.

That same drive pushed him to start his own business despite hearing horror stories of restaurants that had gone belly up before they'd even gotten off the ground. His work ethic, persistence, and passion had made his business what it was. Marigold was a small place, but its culinary scene was just as competitive as other, bigger cities. He had beaten the odds. After the bumpy first year, which he had expected, he'd had nothing but success with Ariana.

He never wanted to get lulled into complacency, though, so he'd kept pushing forward even as Ariana racked up accolades. He wanted to keep striving, to keep climbing to the place where everything in his life was even *more* secure, before taking a break. He had thought he was still on that climb to a resting point, but Grace was making him rethink what a resting point truly looked like. The way he felt about her reminded him of everything he'd set aside in favor of his work.

Joshua tried to focus on the conversation at hand again, but he still felt distracted.

Maybe he had reached the resting point on his climb without realizing it and needed to take that break that Alan had been pushing him to take for a long time. What was the point of building everything he'd built and not taking the time to step back to appreciate everything he had done? When was he going to enjoy his life? He couldn't keep pushing the finish line farther and farther back every time he accomplished something.

"Hey, guys," Grace said, appearing at Joshua's side.

"Hey." Joshua rested his hand on the small of her back and smiled down at her. When she smiled back, it almost felt like a spark of electricity travelled between them. It felt good having her by his side.

No. It felt *great*.

CHAPTER THIRTEEN

"Hey, Mom! Just wanted to let you know I made it to Boston okay and I'm about to pick up Nic," Holly said to Lydia on the phone. "He's just grabbing the last of his stuff."

"Great!" Lydia responded, beaming.

She couldn't wait for Holly and Nic to arrive. They were a little more than a short ferry ride away and were going to stay for a good chunk of the summer to take some much needed time together and recharge before school started up again. Lydia put her laptop to sleep in the inn's back office and started to tidy up some papers as she cradled the phone between her shoulder and her ear.

"I made pretty good time on the drive," Holly

added. "Hopefully it'll be the same on the way to the ferry."

"Fingers crossed." Lydia moved the phone to her other ear, tapping the papers against the desk to straighten them and then filing them away. "What do you guys want to do first when you get here? Maybe take a rest, then go out to dinner?"

"Yeah, that sounds amazing. I don't get how just sitting down in a car can be so tiring, so a nap is definitely in order. And I know I say this every time, but I can't wait to eat something there. Like a good and proper meal that hasn't been sitting under heat lamps in a cafeteria for hours." Holly laughed. "I hope some of our plans involve trying out new restaurants. And re-trying some old favorites."

"You know I wouldn't mind that." Lydia laughed too. She heard the car door opening and Holly saying a muffled *hello*. "Is that Nic?"

"It is," Holly informed her.

"Hi, Lydia," Nic said distantly.

"Hi! I can't wait to see you both. I'll let you guys start driving so I can see you sooner."

"Okay," Holly agreed. "Love you and see you soon."

"Love you too."

Lydia hung up, then headed over to the

innkeeper's residence for lunch with an extra bounce in her step. Just as she got to the front door, Grant's truck pulled up. She waved, waiting for him to reach her so they could walk inside together.

"Hey, Lyds," Grant said as he stepped up to her, giving her a kiss on the lips. "What do you want to do for lunch?"

"I'm not sure. Maybe a salad, or something light like that? I had a heavy breakfast, and Holly and Nic will want to go out to eat when we get here." Lydia stepped inside and shut the door behind Grant. "Or we could make chicken salad and make it into a sandwich for you, then I can have it over this romaine lettuce I need to eat."

"Sounds perfect to me."

The two of them went into the kitchen and got started on lunch, with Grant poaching the chicken breast with some herbs and Lydia chopping up some celery and grapes. Before they could start assembling the salad, Lydia's phone rang again.

"Hold on, it might be Holly." She wiped her hands on a towel and pulled her phone from her pocket. She frowned, though, when she didn't recognize the number. It was a Boston area code.

"Hello?"

"Is this Lydia Walker?" a woman asked, her voice serious.

"Yes, this is her." Lydia swallowed, something in her gut tightening even before the woman said another word.

"This is Dr. Tipper from Boston Medical. I was calling because your daughter Holly has been in an accident."

* * *

Grant watched Lydia's face turn from a confused frown to a look of tense worry, and then to pure shock. Her knees wobbled a little as she leaned against the counter. He rushed over and put his arm around her just in case her knees went out. Her face had gone completely pale.

"Yes, I understand," Lydia said, her voice shaking as much as her hands were. "What happened?"

He couldn't hear what the person was saying on the other end of the line, but it was probably bad. Lydia got even paler, her face nearly white as a sheet. Dread crept up his spine.

"Okay, thank you. We'll be there as soon as possible." She hung up and let her phone clatter onto the countertop.

"What happened?" Grant asked, his chest tight. He ran his hands up and down her arms.

"Holly and Nicolas got into a car accident in Boston. Nicolas is okay and... and Holly will be fine too." Her eyes fluttered closed and she pressed her palm to her chest. "It's all going to be okay."

Even so, Lydia burst into tears. Grant pulled her into his arms and let her cry against his shirt, rubbing her back. The kisses he pressed against her hair weren't much, but he wanted to do anything he could to soothe her. She was trembling all over and took a few moments to pull herself back together.

"We've got to go, then," Grant said softly. "To get to Boston as soon as we can."

She nodded and went to grab her purse, texting Kathy and Angela about what had happened on their way out to Grant's truck. He drove them to the ferry, and fortunately, they didn't have to wait long before they were ushered on board. The timing had worked out well.

Lydia didn't speak much the entire ferry ride over, and Grant made sure to stick close to her side, either holding her hand or putting his arm around her waist.

When she did speak, Grant didn't try to interject or offer her words that he knew wouldn't help.

Instead, he just listened. Her thoughts came out almost as a stream of consciousness, like she was putting down a to-do list of things she had to do when she saw Holly—hugging her, making sure that the doctor had given her enough pain meds, getting instructions on what to do to speed her recovery. Lydia liked spreadsheets and organization, so this didn't surprise him.

When they finally got to the hospital, Grant could feel Lydia's nerves ratchet up another few notches. He completely understood. Just the environment of being in a hospital, with its drab colors and somber air, could make anyone feel nervous. Even though the doctor had said Holly and Nicolas were okay, he knew that Lydia needed to see them to believe it.

"Hi, I'm here to see Holly Walker? I'm her mother," Lydia said when they got to the front desk. "And I'd like to see her boyfriend, Nicolas, too since his family isn't in the area."

"Ah, yes. Please sign in, and I'll show you to her room," the nurse said. "I believe the young man is with her since his injuries weren't as extensive."

They both signed in, and the nurse whisked them to Holly's room. Nicolas was sitting in a chair, a bruise on his cheek and some stitches on his arm, and

Holly was in bed, looking equally banged up. Her dark hair was down around her shoulders in messy tangles, like someone had taken it down from its usual ponytail in haste.

"Holly!" Lydia exclaimed, rushing over and putting her arms around Holly as much as she could in her position. "I'm so glad you're okay. I'm so glad *both* of you are okay."

Lydia gave Nicolas a gentle hug too, tears escaping from her eyes. Even though she was still crying, Grant could see the relief in her eyes. He felt the same way. Holly was almost a daughter to him, and he couldn't imagine what life would be like without her bubbly smile.

CHAPTER FOURTEEN

Angela checked her phone for the tenth time in five minutes, but there wasn't any news from Lydia yet. The last text she'd gotten was Lydia telling her that they'd arrived at the hospital in Boston. Thick tension filled the air, with Kathy and Grace quietly talking at the front desk and Patrick sticking close to Angela.

Usually, with all of them together, someone would inevitably crack a joke or a smile. But if someone tried to lighten the mood in this moment, Angela doubted it would land well. All of them were anxious to hear about how Holly and Nicolas were doing. Angela adored her friend's daughter. Holly was so much like her mother that sometimes speaking to her felt like speaking to Lydia from the past. But the young woman still had her own unique, bright energy. Angela had liked Nicolas the few times she had met him, too. She hoped that both of them would recover from the accident with no issues.

When Angela's phone finally rang, everyone jumped. She answered right away.

"Hey, how are they?" she asked, not wasting time with pleasantries.

"Everyone's okay," Lydia said, her voice a bit faint as it came through the line. Angela sagged with relief and gave a thumbs up to everyone gathered around her. All of them let out a collective breath, looking as relieved as she felt. "Holly has a broken arm, and Nicolas is banged up, plus the car is totaled. But the doctor said it could have been much worse."

Even though everything was okay, Angela could still hear the stress in her friend's voice. She knew the feeling. After her mother had collapsed last summer, the wait to hear whether she was okay, sitting in a sterile hospital waiting room, had been one of the worst experiences of her life.

"We're all glad to hear they're doing okay," Angela said. "Everything is fine here, so don't rush back, okay?"

"Okay." Lydia sniffed and cleared her throat.

"Holly will be released soon, and we'll all take the ferry back."

"All right. We're looking forward to seeing you all."

Angela hung up and told everyone the details. The tension in the air lessened, but Angela knew it would only go away once they could see Holly and Nicolas in person. This situation made Angela miss Jake more than ever, so she excused herself and called Scott to talk to her son.

"Hey, Angela," Scott said in greeting when he answered. "How are you?"

"I'm okay. How are things with you?" Angela genuinely wanted to know. Things were civil between them since the divorce, and she had gotten used to small talk like this. He was going to be part of her life forever, and having an antagonistic relationship wasn't good for anyone.

"Not too bad. A little tired, but you know how it is. Jake never seems to run out of energy." He chuckled. "Want to talk with him?"

"Yes, please. Thanks." Angela waited for Scott to hand over the phone.

"Hi, Mommy!" Jake said after a moment.

"Hey, honey! I just wanted to hear your voice."

Angela said, her eyes welling up with tears at the sound of his sweet voice. She swallowed them back. "How are things with Dad? What have you guys been up to?

"It's so fun! We've been to the zoo a bunch of times and we've watched so many movies and he's teaching me how to throw a football like they do in the NFL." The words came out in one excited breath, making Angela smile despite the overload of emotions she was feeling—an odd mix of sadness that he wasn't with her and gratitude that he was happy and healthy.

"That sounds amazing!" She kept her voice upbeat despite the tears that dripped down her cheeks. She didn't want Jake to worry about her or think she was sad. "What kinds of animals did you see at the zoo?"

"They had lions and tigers and stuff, but I've seen those before." Jake sounded so over them that she had to chuckle. "But they had red pandas and they were doing cool stuff. And llamas! And kangaroos. I got to pet one."

"Wow, you did? That's so cool." And much better than the last zoo she'd taken him to, which was under construction.

"Daddy took a picture of me and this kangaroo

who really liked me. You could just walk around and hang out with them."

He told her more about what they were doing until he and Scott had to head out to play soccer with some of his old friends from school.

"Love you, Mommy," Jake said.

"Love you too. Miss you. Put your dad on the phone again, please," Angela requested. There was a shuffling sound, and soon Scott was back on the line. "He sounds happy," she told her ex.

"He is. He's always upbeat. It's a nice change of pace," Scott agreed.

"I bet. Can you send me the pictures you took of him and the kangaroos you guys saw?"

"Yeah, of course. I'll send them right after we hang up, plus some other ones. Talk to you later."

"Thanks. Talk soon." Angela hung up before she let a couple more tears slip from her eyes.

A few moments later, a few photos came through via text. Jake was grinning as he stood near a small kangaroo, who was very interested in the little boy's shoelaces. There were a few others of Jake in front of other exhibits, including the red pandas that he'd loved so much. His grin was wide, showing off the little gap where his grown-up tooth was still growing in.

Angela sniffed, wiping away her tears. Scott really knew how to give their son a fun experience, one he couldn't get back in Marigold. That made her feel a tiny bit more at ease, but still, her heart ached. She couldn't wait for Jake to return.

"Hey," Patrick said softly from the doorway. When he saw Angela's face, he crossed the room and put his arms around her, pulling her close. "Everything okay?"

"Yeah. I just miss Jake." She showed Patrick the photos of her little boy at the zoo.

"He looks like he's having a lot of fun," Patrick said. "But I understand that it's still hard. He'll be back before you know it."

Angela leaned against him and sighed, grateful that he was there. He always knew just the right words to put her at ease.

* * *

Logically, Lydia recognized that the odds of anything else happening to Holly and Nicolas on the short walk to the car and the short cab ride to the ferry were low, but that hadn't stopped her from glancing at them often during the drive. She found herself doing the exact same thing now that they were at the ferry port.

Holly and Nic got seated on the ferry, settled across from Lydia and Grant with their hands threaded together and bodies huddled close. Holly's broken arm was in a sling, so Nicolas was taking extra care to not jostle her.

As the ferry pulled off, Lydia began sorting through all of the logistics that came along with the crash: the insurance, the car, Holly's medication, and the instructions her doctor had given her to take care of her cast. She had told Holly not to worry about the car—at the end of the day, the insurance was going to cover everything since the other driver was at fault, and she could always get another one. The only thing that mattered was that she and Nicolas were okay.

The care of Holly's cast seemed simple enough too. Lydia had the motherly urge to jump in and help her daughter with things, but she knew that Holly wouldn't tolerate that for more than a day or two.

Lydia added a few things to her to-do list and looked at Holly and Nicolas again. They were talking quietly, their heads bowed together. Nic gently rubbed Holly's good arm before giving it a gentle squeeze. Both of them were still a little pale and on edge, but they were helping each other through it. Lydia was glad to see it—being an emotional support was important and they seemed to be good for each other in that regard. Back when she'd been Holly's age, most guys hadn't seemed to be as attuned to their girlfriends' emotional needs as Nic was.

Once they arrived back on Marigold, Grant took the drive from the ferry to the inn carefully, staying a few miles per hour under the speed limit and checking his mirrors twice. When they reached the inn, Kathy, Angela, Grace, and Patrick greeted them with open arms. The relief on their faces was obvious.

"We're so glad you two are okay," Angela said, giving Holly a one-armed hug before moving on to Nicolas.

"Thanks. We're glad too," Holly said with a shaky smile.

Everyone got their hugs and well-wishes in before leaving them to get settled in. Grant and Lydia took Holly and Nicolas to the innkeeper's residence and helped them put their bags away. Then Nicolas headed out to the living room, talking with Grant about his past semester, leaving Holly and Lydia alone in the guest room. Holly sat on the bed, gently rubbing at her cast.

"Do you need any pain meds?" Lydia asked, her brows furrowing.

"No, I think I'm good. It's just a little itchy already." Holly laughed lightly. "It's like when Jake had his cast on and he couldn't reach his itch. He tried to stick a pencil in there to reach. I don't think that's in the doctor's care notes."

"That must be incredibly annoying." Lydia remembered how Jake had tried and tried to get to an itchy spot on his wrist when he'd had a cast on, to no avail. It had driven the active little boy nuts.

"It is." Holly didn't move from the bed, pursing her lips as if something else was on her mind.

"What's up, Hols?" Lydia sat down next to her.

"Nic and I were talking on the ferry. He's decided to transfer again. He's going to come up to Syracuse so we can be closer together. He might have to take some summer classes if all of his credits don't transfer, but he's fine with that," Holly said softly. "I know it's a huge step, but we want to be closer to each other. We're in love with each other and the accident only showed us that we can't take things for granted. Why not make it happen since we have the opportunity?"

Lydia nodded and gave Holly a hug, taking care to not bump her broken arm. Sometimes Holly surprised her with how mature she was. She and Nic weren't just moving to be closer for the rest of their time in college. It seemed like they were thinking years and years ahead, visualizing what they wanted their future to look like.

"That's true." Lydia gave Holly's good arm a squeeze. "Those are very wise words."

Lydia just wished she hadn't come to that conclusion so viscerally, but she was so glad that Holly was okay.

CHAPTER FIFTEEN

Grace woke up without an alarm clock, rolling over and stretching in her comfortable bed. Her father's urn caught her eye as she did. It sat on top of her dresser, greeting her every morning as she woke up when her room began to fill with soft light.

She had been in Marigold for about a month by now, and the slow, friendly pace of the island had seeped into her bones. She hadn't had any mornings where she'd woken up in a panic that she'd forgotten to do something in a while.

She hopped out of bed and got dressed, falling into her new morning routine of saying hello to Lydia and Angela and getting some breakfast. Today's special pastry was a chocolate chip banana muffin, which Grace grabbed and paired with some fruit. As she ate, Lydia gave her an update on Holly and Nicolas, who were doing much better. Grace was glad to hear it. Even though she had just met Holly, she had come to like her a lot.

Falling back into her friendship with Angela and Lydia had felt so easy, and they had gotten just as close as they'd been as teenagers without much effort. Being able to casually chat with them every day had made her so much happier in so many little ways. They always had a joke to share or an interesting story to tell. Half of Grace's jaunts around town were inspired by her friends, who seemed to know every nook and cranny of the island.

Pretty much everything in Marigold had made her happier than she had been in the months before coming on this trip, like she had thrown a warm-toned filter on her view of life. The future looked bright and filled with possibility.

After finishing her morning muffin, Grace headed out to the rec center for another class that she had been looking forward to—an introduction to golf. She and Joshua had made plans to take it after the great time they had at Patrick's book signing, and she couldn't wait to see him again and learn more about the sport.

She hadn't played much golf in her life. It was

the kind of sport that required a lot of time that she never had. Her dad was a big golfer before he got sick, though. He used to take her out to the range when she was little, letting her pretend to drive the little golf cart around. This afternoon was going to be a double bonus for her—she would get to revisit a good memory of her father and she would get to spend time with Joshua.

"Hi there!" Grace said, waving at Joshua when he walked up to the rec center.

"Hi!" Joshua gave her a hug. She couldn't help but feel the spark between them again. It happened every time they touched, and it was an addictive sort of feeling. "I can't believe you talked me into golf."

"You didn't require that much prodding." Grace gently poked his side. "Though I'm a little surprised to see the golf attire."

Joshua was wearing a green striped polo and khakis. He was usually a button-down shirt or t-shirt and jeans kind of guy, very casual, so it was an interesting change. Of course, he still looked handsome. Grace's cheeks flushed as they always did when she looked at him.

"I know. I forgot I even had this stuff in my closet." He pulled at the shirt, smiling. "If I showed up to the restaurant in this, my team would probably think the *real* me had been abducted by aliens."

Soon, the entire class had gathered. The instructor, an older bald man named Richard, gave them a quick primer of the clubs and basic rules. On their walk over, he explained a few more things about the golf course and the history of the sport, gesturing wildly as if golf were as thrilling and dangerous as military history. Grace had to smile. Richard had to be the most enthusiastic golf historian in the state, not that there were a lot of people in that category.

When they got to the course, Richard took them to a practice area and showed them how to putt and drive. Once everyone got the hang of it, he left them to practice.

"Maybe we should have started with mini-golf," Grace joked as she putted and missed the hole by about a foot.

"I don't think that would have helped." Joshua putted his ball and missed too, shrugging. "But whatever, it's all about the fun."

"True. And speaking of fun, I had so much fun at Ariana the other week. I'm still thinking about it."

"Yeah?" he smiled, resting his hand on his putter's handle.

"Oh yeah. I'm still thinking about... well, all of it. But that unusual pasta—fregola, or whatever it was called? So good."

"Yeah, the fregola di mare? I'm glad to hear it made such a good impression. I've loved the dish ever since I first tried it in Italy, and I don't see it on restaurant menus often." His smile broadened. "And the restaurant is my baby, so I only want the best for it."

"It made an amazing impression. I'll need to go back sometime and try another one of the specials."

"You should." He picked up his ball, but didn't place it again. "I've been planning to open another restaurant in Boston or maybe other cities, so maybe Ariana will have a sibling someday, so to speak."

"Really? That's great!"

"It is. It's going to be a lot of work, though. I might have to go back and forth to Boston a lot, or I might even move there to get the restaurant off the ground." He finally put the ball in place again.

It took a few seconds, but then his words clicked in Grace's brain. There was a chance he wouldn't be around the island much longer. Or there was a good chance he'd only be around every once in a while. For some reason, that thought made a little bubble of sadness rise in her chest.

"But the non-food part is a bit dull sometimes," Joshua continued, unaware of her inner thoughts. "It makes me glad I didn't go into construction or finance, not that those ever tempted me. I don't want to bore you with all that," he added with a chuckle. "How are things with you at the inn?"

"Good! Relaxing. I haven't slept this much in years," she said, shaking her head a little to clear it and setting up a putt again. She had forgotten all the details of posture that Richard had gone through already, but she tapped the ball toward the practice hole anyway. "I've just been soaking it all in and trying to figure out what's next. It's such a big change from life back in Colorado."

"What was life in Colorado like?" he asked as her ball made it into the hole. "Nice shot."

"Thanks! Pure luck." Grace laughed. "Living in Colorado was completely different. It was beautiful, just like here, but the people seemed to move faster. People were very outdoorsy, too, which was nice when I got the chance to explore with my camera. I could ask a total stranger what hiking trails were great and get a recommendation. But mostly I was caring for my dad."

"I see." Joshua nodded. "I bet that was difficult too."

"It was," Grace said. "It was a twenty-four-seven gig, and I had to coordinate a lot of moving parts—his medicines, doctor's appointments, food, all that. But I'm glad I got to spend time with him before he passed. He used to take me to this golf course when I was little, actually, so I'm getting to revisit memories of him while I learn something new."

"It must be nice to visit home again."

"It is. It's been the perfect place to reset before diving back into life, you know?" She looked out onto the other people in the class, who were much more focused than they were on learning how to play golf. For a moment, she wondered what life beyond Marigold would look like.

"Marigold really is that kind of place. It's nice to be in a place where you can know your neighbors but you can do a lot of things." Joshua turned his putter around on its end. "Whenever I talk to friends from out of town, they're genuinely surprised at all the things you can do in a weekend out here."

"I know! It's great. A lot of the perks of a city without all the bad parts," she said.

"That should be Marigold's new motto." He laughed.

"I'll call the tourism department and let them know." Grace smiled.

By the end of the class, Grace wasn't much better at golf as she had been when she'd come in, and neither was Joshua. They had spent most of their time chatting and joking around, but the thought of whatever was between them lingered in the back of her mind. Could this spark between them turn into something more? She wasn't sure she was ready for anything to happen, but at the same time, her attraction to him was stronger than ever.

If she had to put together her ideal man, Joshua would be it. He was dedicated to his passions without taking himself so seriously that he was a bore. Jokes popped from his mouth almost faster than Grace could keep up with. And he loved food, just like she did. Talking with him felt so easy, too, as if he could pick up on whatever wavelength she was putting out and vice versa.

They left the driving range, falling into step with one another.

"Let me walk you to your car," Joshua said, gently resting a hand on her back.

"Thank you."

She glanced up at him, admiring his strong jaw and the graying hair on his temples that made him look distinguished and handsome. He had a few smile lines in the corners of his eyes, though he also had some worry lines between his brows, probably from all of his hard work on his business. He'd dedicated years to something besides his love life, just like she had to her father.

Was it too late for them to change gears and to make space for something that was just for them?

They stopped at Grace's rental car, neither of them making a move to leave. Grace had her key fob in her hand, but she didn't unlock the vehicle, and Joshua didn't turn to head for his car. They just looked at each other for a few moments. Some hesitation filled his eyes, and she was sure he could probably see the same in hers. But then something shifted, as if some unseen force had pulled away the barrier between them, and Joshua took her hand. He took one more step nearer to her, closing the space between them, and dropped his head, pressing his lips to hers.

They kissed so softly and sweetly that Grace felt a warmth she hadn't experienced in ages spread all through her body, from her head to her toes. She threaded her fingers between Joshua's, savoring the connection.

CHAPTER SIXTEEN

Hunter squeezed one of Scratch's many cat toys and made a kissy sound to grab the little black cat's attention. Scratch lifted his head from where he was napping on the floor and lazily got to his feet, stretching into an arch. By the time the kitten made it over to the couch, Hunter had switched to a feather duster toy that Scratch had been loving for the past few weeks.

Hunter half-smiled as Scratch jumped for the toy, his little belly wobbling as he moved. Scratch had been a scrawny little kitten when Brooke had first found him outside of her old apartment, but now he was adorably chunky. It was impossible to resist sneaking him a little piece of chicken or fish whenever he let out a sad meow.

Scratch skidded across the floor, chirping in annoyance that the toy had gotten away from him again. Hunter teased him a little more before sighing. He knew he was procrastinating. After helping Brooke at the bakery this morning, he had come home and done some research for the role he was going to be taking on next year in a new film. It was exciting, but once he'd gotten to the point of watching short documentaries on the food during the time period the movie was set in, he'd decided to take a break before his brain overloaded.

Now he just had to build up the courage to check off the last thing on his list for the day.

"Bored already?" Hunter asked Scratch, who had stopped going for the toy and started grooming his face. He gave the toy one more wave before tossing it aside and sitting back on the couch. "Well, I guess that's the end of my procrastinating."

He patted his lap, and Scratch hopped up, kneading his paws a little bit before settling down. After petting Scratch right above his tail for a moment, Hunter took a deep breath and grabbed his phone, dialing Brooke's parents' home phone number.

"Hello?" Mitch's deep voice came through the line as he answered.

"Hi, Mitch, It's Hunter."

"Oh, hey, Hunter! How are you?"

"Good, good. I'm glad I caught you—I was actually hoping to talk to Phoebe as well." Hunter rested his hand on Scratch's back, letting the soft sound of the cat's purring soothe his nerves a bit.

"No problem. Just a second." There was some movement on the other end of the line. Then Mitch's voice came through again, sounding a bit more distant this time. "You're on speaker phone."

"Hi, Hunter!" Phoebe said with just as much warmth as her husband had. "What's up?"

He took another deep breath and decided to cut to the chase. "I'm in love with Brooke, and I just wanted to ask for your blessing in asking her to marry me. I wanted to do this right."

Hunter closed his eyes, wishing he could have said it more gracefully and not just blurted it out like that, but he had gotten his point across. How could he put his feelings for Brooke into words, anyway? He hoped he showed it every way he could. He'd do anything for her.

The line went silent for a moment. The pause was killing him, sweat collecting on his palms and his heart pounding. This was more nervous than he had felt at any audition by miles. But in some ways, it *was* an audition for the role of being Brooke's eventual husband and a member of their family.

Being famous had made it hard for him to form relationships on both sides. Sometimes he doubted people's motivations for getting close to him, especially other actors. When he'd first started in Hollywood, he'd had no idea just how far some people would go to advance their own careers, even to the point of exploiting or betraying other people. All of the stories he'd been told about the cutthroat acting world hadn't come close to capturing how gutted he had felt when he realized that someone he'd considered a friend was anything but.

On the flip side, sometimes people doubted Hunter's sincerity, since they thought he was all Hollywood and fake. As much as it hurt, he understood that because of his own experiences with being used. Connecting to friends he could count on, who felt they could count on him in return, was a difficult task.

But Marigold had proven to be different. People had been a little surprised and starstruck by him at first, but now he felt like he could be himself. There wasn't the artificial glamour of Hollywood here—the residents of Marigold were just regular people like

Brooke's family, enjoying their lives and forming healthy relationships.

Hunter had gotten close to Phoebe, Mitch, Angela, and Travis in the time he and Brooke had been together, and he knew they were truly kind people. He just hoped they felt the same way about him. None of them had ever suggested otherwise, but that didn't ease his nerves at the moment. Anxiety and reason weren't natural companions.

Phoebe finally let out a noise that sounded like a soft sob, but Hunter couldn't quite tell until Mitch spoke.

"We'd love to give our blessing," Mitch said, his voice thick with emotion. "We're overjoyed that you've made Brooke so happy."

"We see her face when she looks at you," Phoebe added, sniffing. "And it's so clear you two are a perfect match."

Hunter resisted the urge to pump his fist in the air so he wouldn't disturb the now-sleeping Scratch. "I'm so glad. And I feel the same way. I've never met a woman quite like Brooke."

"I'm so excited!" Phoebe's voice sounded a little clearer, her excitement overriding the first wave of strong emotion. "Gosh, now we have to keep this secret. I promise not to let it slip."

"You won't have to keep it quiet for too long," Hunter promised. "I'm not going to sit on this. I'm really excited too."

"Good, because I'm not sure how long I could keep this secret either." Mitch laughed. "We're thrilled for you to officially join our family."

"I am too." Hunter couldn't keep the smile off his face. "Thank you both."

"You're welcome, hun," Phoebe said.

Hunter hung up and scooped Scratch into his arms, getting to his feet. The cat was a little startled, but he settled down when Hunter held him close and rocked him, almost like they were dancing. Being the loving little kitten that he was, Scratch picked up on Hunter's joy and started to purr.

"Step one is done," Hunter murmured, kissing Scratch on the head. "Now I just have to figure out how to actually pop the question."

Scratch looked up at him and meowed as if he understood everything Hunter had just said. The sight of the little cat's face gave Hunter an idea. He smiled to himself and put Scratch down, picking up his phone to make a few more calls.

* * *

The gentle hum of activity in the innkeeper's residence perked Angela up as she cooked dinner with Lydia. It was a full house at the inn with Holly and Nicolas in town, plus the constant flow of friends and family she was used to. It was a nice change of pace to have the two young adults around, even as they both recovered from their accident.

"Can you hand me the heavy cream?" Angela asked Lydia.

"Yup, just a second." Her friend tapped a few things on her phone before going to grab the heavy cream. She sighed as she passed it over. "I feel like insurance companies make things difficult for you just for fun at this point."

"Still struggling with that?" Angela asked.

"Not struggling, no, but sitting on hold and emailing back and forth." Lydia set down her phone so she could wash her hands, then dried them on a kitchen towel. "The good news is that the adjuster took a look, and the other driver's insurance should pay for it because he was at fault."

"That is good news! Sounds like the insurance nightmare is almost over." Angela poured a bit of heavy cream into the sauce she was whipping up.

"Yeah." Lydia glanced out the window to where Holly, Nicolas, and Jake were kicking around a soccer ball and laughing. "And it seems like they're both on the mend."

Angela looked out the window too, following her friend's gaze. Even with her broken arm, Holly was running around, kicking the ball gently toward Jake. Nicolas put his hand on her back and said something that made Holly laugh and look up at him with warm affection in her eyes. Angela smiled and went back to whisking her sauce.

It was sweet to see how Nicolas had taken care of Holly as she recovered from the accident, getting up to grab things and checking in to see if she needed painkillers. Even if Lydia hadn't told Angela that the two of them were getting really serious, Angela could have guessed.

"They're very sweet," she said, nodding toward Holly and Nicolas.

"They are." Lydia sighed, a tinge of a smile on her lips. "It's a little scary since Holly's still my baby, but Nicolas is a great boyfriend."

"Yeah, he is," Angela said. She momentarily wondered what life would be like when Jake was Holly's age. She knew she would feel just like Lydia did when he started dating someone seriously—an odd mix of worry, pride, and confusion as to where the time had gone.

"Oh, by the way, Grant asked me about my move into his place," Lydia said, putting some chicken on a piping hot pan. "We still need to get some details nailed down so I can move right in after the wedding or right before."

"That's great!"

"Yeah! We'll have to figure things out with Kathy too, since she'll probably have to take on more responsibilities. I'll be close enough to help with emergencies, and you'll still be here, of course." Lydia poked at the chicken with a spatula. "And once I leave, Patrick could move into the innkeeper's residence. I bet he could rent out his current house easily."

Angela found a small spoon and scooped up some of her sauce, offering it to Lydia. Lydia gave her a thumbs up once she tasted it and went back to her work.

"Yeah, his house would be a great rental. It's in a great location."

"It is. And Jennifer would totally help with the listing. It seems like this whole moving thing could be more seamless than I thought." Lydia poked a thermometer into a piece of chicken and nodded when she read the gauge indicating it had reached the right temperature.

"I'll miss having you as a taste tester, though," Angela said. "It'll be so weird to not live with you after more than a year of this. It feels like the default at this point."

"Yeah." Lydia's green eyes got a little misty. "It'll always be one of the most special times of my life."

"Same." Angela felt tears well up in her own eyes, and she cleared her throat.

Being able to have moments like this so often with one of her best friends wouldn't have happened without Marigold. She hadn't lived with anyone but Scott for ages, so she had forgotten how fun it could be. Lydia was always up for watching the trashy, goofy TV shows that Patrick politely declined to watch, and of course, they had these amazing dinners.

She wanted to take the next step with Patrick, and Lydia was always going to be around. But it was going to be an adjustment for sure.

They hugged, holding on to each other for a few beats before breaking apart and laughing.

"We're so sappy sometimes, huh?" Angela chuckled.

"Yeah. I can't even deny it."

Lydia went back to cooking, and so did Angela, their conversation moving on to other topics. But even as it did, that warm, happy ache remained in Angela's chest. What her friend had said was true, and Angela felt the exact same way. She was always going to look back on this year as the one where her life changed for the better.

* * *

Joshua took a left turn instead of a right one, drumming his fingers on his steering wheel. The right turn would have gotten him to his restaurant faster, but the left turn went along the most scenic part of the island lined with many of the trees that he'd learned about during his nature walk class. He rolled down the windows to let the fresh sea air come in, its salty scent lifting his spirits. It was a beautiful summer day, bordering on slightly too hot without the breeze.

He slowed to a stop at a sign, and since no one was around, he looked around a little. Everywhere he looked was beautiful—the lush greenery, the colorful birds peeking out through the trees, the clear blue sky and dark blue ocean blending at the horizon far off in the distance. It reminded him of how lucky he was to live there.

A car pulled up behind him and honked,

prompting him to move forward. He made another turn to head toward the restaurant, sighing. Some days his go-go-go attitude didn't mesh with Marigold's calm, quiet beauty, and he was noticing that split more and more often lately. Maybe he needed to slow down a bit. Did he really need to open a new restaurant in Boston? Or anywhere else, really?

He ran a hand through his hair as a few buildings came into view. Ariana was very well established here, and he loved everything about the restaurant—its location, its food, its guests. Did he want to put just as much time and effort into building a restaurant like Ariana in a big city that couldn't come close to being as beautiful as Marigold, or did he want to put that energy somewhere else?

Besides, maybe the experience of opening a new place would be different for him now that he was older. He was well aware of how much more rest he needed now that he was taking it.

When he reached his restaurant, he parked in the back and went inside, taking a sip of coffee from his travel mug.

"What's up?" Alan asked when Joshua passed by him in the kitchen. "You're in later than usual this morning. You okay?"

"Yeah, I was just taking the scenic route and started thinking about the Boston restaurant. I don't... I don't know if it's the right move. I think I need to slow down. I can't run myself into the ground anymore."

Alan's eyes widened. He stared at Joshua for a moment, then broke into a grin. "Wow, is this a sign of the apocalypse? The workaholic doesn't want to push for the next bigger, better thing?"

Joshua rolled his eyes and leaned up against a prep table. "I'm not going to stop completely. I'm just going to pursue some other things."

"I'm happy to hear that. You should get after those dreams that have been lingering in the back of your head," Alan said.

"Yeah." He let out a soft sigh and looked around the kitchen. As always, the kitchen staff was running like a well-oiled machine, even without Alan standing there over everyone. "Now that I've freed my headspace from all the plans for the restaurant, I have more space to think."

"But ideas can be addictive. The kind of thing to get you through the rough parts of your day." Alan tucked his hands into his pockets. "I've thought about opening a restaurant of my own one day, and sometimes I whip up some new dish that I would put on my dream menu."

Joshua nodded, sipping his coffee. He had tried Alan's food time and time again over the years, but mostly when he was creating ideas for specials. The parameters weren't tight—usually Joshua gave him guidance on the protein he wanted or the price range he had to stay within—but they were there. Alan was a talented chef. Who knew what he could do if he had free rein?

An idea hit Joshua so dead-on that he wondered why he hadn't thought of it sooner.

"Or you could be the one to go to Boston and open up the second restaurant as a partner," Joshua said.

"Really?" Alan went completely still, as though he was worried the opportunity might disappear if he made any sudden movements.

"Yeah. And I could stay here and manage this location." The wheels in Joshua's brain started spinning. "Connor's an amazing sous chef, and he could step in for you. He knows the ropes, and he's more than ready."

It made so much sense. He trusted Alan, and this would allow both of them to get what they wanted. Alan could achieve his dream of opening a restaurant, and Joshua could appreciate what he had here in Marigold, taking things a little slower. Plus, Alan probably had some great, fresh ideas for the direction the restaurant could go. Italian-inspired food was Joshua's wheelhouse, but there were a lot of ways to put a twist on it.

"I'm in." Alan gave a decisive nod, his eyes gleaming with enthusiasm. "I'm definitely in. Tell me what you're thinking. Let's talk about it."

Joshua grinned. "This is why I know we should be in business together. I can't think of anyone else in the world who would dive into this with the same gusto you will."

He clapped his friend on the shoulder, and the two men shared a look, both of them smiling broadly. Then Alan whipped out a notebook and a pen, starting to jot down notes as Joshua talked out some of his ideas.

CHAPTER SEVENTEEN

Grace framed a shot of a field and snapped a photo, then stepped aside to show Kathy. They had gone out to some of the spots Grace had been to during her nature walk so that she could show Kathy a few photography techniques.

The view was beautiful, expanding out toward the ocean with only a few trees in the way. Grace recognized some sassafras and some other plants, which she pointed out to Kathy as they snapped photos.

"Oh, I see what you mean!" Kathy said when Grace pointed out what she had done with her last shot. "Wow, that seems like such a simple fix!"

"I know, right? When I learned it, I never went back to doing it the old way," Grace said.

"I'm so glad we finally got to come out here and do this." Kathy took her camera back and looked through the photos they had taken.

"Same here."

Grace and Kathy had been talking about going out to exchange photography tips and tricks ever since Grace's arrival on the island, and they were finally doing it. Grace loved Kathy's work. It was fun and eclectic, much different than Grace's. She played with color and captured views and angles that Grace would have never thought of.

"Can you show me how you created the effect you used in that seagull photo?" Grace asked.

"Yeah, of course! Want to keep walking to find a new spot?" Kathy suggested.

"Sure, why not?"

The two of them gathered their cameras and gear before moving on. They were close enough to the ocean that Grace could smell the salt in the air, and the sun was beaming down on her shoulders. Over the past few weeks, she had gotten tanner than she'd been in years—within reason of course. Sunscreen was always in her bag.

"Oh, wow! I can't believe I've never noticed this area before," Grace said when they came across a small clearing. It was almost circular, like a small cul-de-sac in the middle of a forested area. Mushrooms were peppered around the edges. "I was just nearby here for my class, too."

"Yeah, Marigold has so many little spots like this." Kathy put her bag down on a stump and looked around. "Oh, it's a fairy circle! How cool."

"A fairy circle?" Grace pulled her camera out again.

"Yeah. They're natural circles of mushrooms like this, and they look kind of like little seats for fairies to have chats." Kathy grinned. "This totally fits with that fantasy project I'm working on."

"I've never heard it called that before." Grace slowly walked around the circle. "So cool."

"Mushrooms are cool in general." Kathy squatted down next to the stump. "Like they're all connected underground. I bore my family with mushroom facts whenever we have dinner, so stop me if you get tired of hearing about them."

"No, tell me more! My exposure to them ends at eating them and knowing that I shouldn't just eat them straight from the ground even if I *think* I know what they are."

"Let me show you that photography technique first."

Grace showed Kathy how she created the effect

she'd used in one of her photos, then both of them tried it out in the circle. Grace was pleased with how it came out and couldn't wait to fiddle around with the image in Photoshop later.

Once they finished up in the fairy circle, they moved on to the next spot, the two of them chatting about mushrooms and any other topics that came to mind as they captured the beautiful landscape of the island. Once they got closer to town, they photographed some people and some of the buildings at various angles.

Grace didn't know Kathy as well as she knew Lydia and Angela, but they got along really well. It had been a while since she'd gotten to connect with another photographer, period, much less one with a similar sense of humor and a lot of interesting ideas to share. Talking with the youthful and exuberant red-head made the day fly by.

Every photo they took reminded Grace of how much she'd missed the island and how much she liked it here. Colorado was amazing and beautiful too, but something about Marigold was different. The idea of leaving made her heart sink.

Before she knew it, they were back at the inn.

"Thanks so much for everything," Kathy said, putting her camera bag down.

"Thanks to you too! I had a lot of fun." Grace gave the other woman a quick hug before heading upstairs to her room to upload her photos to her computer.

As she transferred them over, she sat back in her chair and sighed. She hadn't had such a productive, creative day in a long time. Marigold had so many beautiful places to capture. She could build up her photography business anywhere; she didn't *have* to be in Colorado to take and sell pictures. Maybe she could start her business up again in Marigold, both selling her pieces and taking photos for people.

Feeling a rush of excitement, Grace finished uploading her shots and packed up her laptop into its little carrying case. Then she trotted downstairs and out to her car, looking up the directions to Nicole Howard's gallery on the way. The two had met at Patrick's book signing, and Nicole had told Grace to stop by at some point. Now seemed like as good a time as any.

It didn't take her long to reach the place, and she parked on the street and headed inside.

"Hey, how are you?" Nicole asked with a big smile when Grace came into the gallery. "I'm so glad you stopped by!"

"I'm good. How are you?"

"Not bad! What brings you in?"

Grace looked around at the gallery, which had an eclectic mix of pieces. All of them were beautiful and unique, from the sculptures to the massive paintings lining the back wall. But somehow, they all fit together. It was similar to Nicole's outfit, which Grace loved. The statuesque woman had mixed two different patterns on her blouse and cardigan, but instead of clashing, it looked cool on her.

"I was hoping to show you some of my pieces, actually, to see if they might be a good fit for the gallery. Do you have a minute?" Grace asked.

"Yeah, totally! Come on back to my office."

Grace's heart rate picked up as they walked toward the back and settled in Nicole's small office. It was packed with art, too, although Grace wasn't sure if it was Nicole's personal art or if the room was doubling as a storage space.

"Let me see what you have," Nicole said, turning so that she could see Grace's laptop as Grace drew it out of the bag and set it on the desk to open it.

She pulled up a series of pieces that she had taken early in her visit to Marigold of various birds and people interacting with them on the boardwalk. There was an old woman feeding some seagulls, some children chasing a pigeon, and a couple eyeing a flock as they ate something. They all captured the birds' movement and the energy of the boardwalk well, at least in Grace's opinion.

Grace waited, her palms going sweaty as Nicole looked through them all. Sharing her work always made her nervous, but now the pressure felt especially high. Selling some pieces would help her income quite a bit, and this was the only high-quality gallery in the area.

Nicole nodded as she looked through everything, her expression hard to read. Grace looked down at her lap instead of staring.

"Wow, these are great! We can definitely work something out," Nicole said after several moments, her whole face brightening.

Grace grinned so widely that she knew her cheeks would hurt later. "Really?"

"Definitely."

* * *

"We're heading out to the beach, Mom!" Holly called out as she headed for the door of the inn with Nicolas behind her. They were both in beachwear, sunglasses, and flip-flops.

"Wait, sunscreen. I don't think we have it." Nicolas gently squeezed Holly's shoulders.

"I have some behind the desk," Lydia said, opening the drawer of the front desk and pulling out the mostly full bottle. "Here you go."

"Thanks! Wouldn't want to get a sunburn with this cast." Holly laughed and tucked the sunscreen into her bag. "What would that even be called? A reverse farmer's tan? Or just a cast tan?"

"A reverse farmer's tan sounds funnier." Nicolas laughed too.

"Have fun, you guys," Lydia told them, waving as they finally slipped out the door.

She was glad to see they were both doing so well. The more she got to know Nicolas, the more she liked him. He was sweet although a little shy, and once he warmed up, he was great to talk to.

It was fun having them around, the two of them making jokes or telling Lydia something she had never known about. It always surprised her how much she missed out on pop culture-wise, although some of the things that Holly and Nicolas liked bewildered her. Maybe this was how her parents had felt when she'd talked their ears off about the cool new trends when she was her daughter's age.

About half an hour later, Lydia put up a sign telling any guests that came by that she was in the common room and headed there for their first book club meeting. Angela was there, putting out some pastries from Brooke's Bakery, while Brooke set up some chairs nearby. It was the perfect space for the book club group, which had grown much larger than the small group that they had initially set out to create. Lydia couldn't wait.

Everyone started to trickle in a few minutes later. There were the women from the business owners' group—Nicole, Leah, and Cora—plus Millie and a few other people who they had all invited. Grace came too, the historical romance they'd picked out as their first read tucked under one arm. She held a bag filled with fruit in her free hand.

"I brought some wine!" Millie declared, holding up a bottle of red.

"And I brought some charcuterie. A perfect match!" Cora added, putting the platter she had brought down on the snack table.

"Oh man, I was supposed to have dinner with my husband later." Nina, one of Millie's friends, gave a playful groan. "Now I'm going to fill up on snacks."

"Sometimes snacks are the best meal, especially with charcuterie and wine," Lydia said, making room for everyone else's snacks too.

Soon the snack table was loaded up with everything from cookies to crackers to soft cheese and fruit. Everyone got themselves some snacks and wine before settling into the circle of chairs that Brook had set up. There was just enough room for everyone.

"Welcome to our first book club meeting! Thanks for coming," Angela said, propping her book on her lap and resting her hands on the top of it. "So, where do we want to start? Maybe some general thoughts?"

"I really liked it," Leah said right away, running her hand over her book's cover. "It wasn't too stuffy, and I didn't feel like I had to look up any of the historical figures to understand what was going on. Admittedly, my grasp on British history is limited."

"Same here, but I don't think anyone is reading a romance wishing for every detail to be historically accurate," Britney, one of Leah's friends, said with a laugh. Then she blushed a little. "I wasn't excited to start reading it since I've only read modern romance stories, but it was really fun. I loved how the duke and Lady Margaret finally realized that they needed each other, even though they never wanted to fall in love in the first place."

"I wanted to smack Duke Remington, though," Lydia interjected. "About ten times at least."

"I'd say at least twenty or thirty times." Nicole's nose wrinkled. "He was a jerk more often than he was sweet. I know that's a thing—the hero being a jerk before the heroine softens him up—but seriously. I get that there were a lot of social norms that we definitely wouldn't follow today, but he was a duke, and he was that *rude*?"

A few others nodded in agreement, including Lydia. She smiled to herself. Grant had gotten such a detailed play by play of her annoyance with the duke as she'd read beside him on the couch that he could have come to the book club without having read the actual book.

"I just chalked that up to fantasy. Like out of all the people this wealthy and powerful guy knew, Margaret was the one to finally tame him," a woman whose name escaped Lydia said. "I definitely wouldn't accept that kind of behavior in real life, though."

"Definitely not!" Millie laughed. "But then again, we probably wouldn't want to live through an alien invasion or see a Godzilla-esque monster, but we'd love to read or watch that over and over again. A duke who's a jerk is much less of a threat."

"Can I say something as a fan of historical romances? I want to know why there are so many dukes! Every hero seems to be a duke," Cora commented with a laugh. "There were like, less than forty in this era according to my less-than-thorough Googling on the subject. Why not a baron, or a viscount or whatever? They were still pretty well off, despite not having as much social clout as a duke."

"Well, it's kind of like dating a millionaire or billionaire or something, but with a lot more baggage and duties, no?" Millie asked, pursing her lips thoughtfully.

"True." Cora nodded. "And this makes me feel old, but I remember when millionaire romances were the big deal. Now it's all billionaires."

"And there are *way* more billionaires in romances than there are in real life," Grace pointed out. "And very few of them have deep, soulful eyes, or perfect abs."

Everyone laughed, which kept the ball rolling steadily for the rest of the meeting. Lydia sipped her wine and enjoyed the lively conversation, glancing over at Angela as her friend shared her own thoughts on the book and everyone else nodded along.

She was so grateful for the community they'd built. They had made this place feel like a true home.

CHAPTER EIGHTEEN

"Hey, are you free?" Joshua asked Grace the moment she picked up the phone, before he even said hello.

"I am." She could hear a mischievous grin in his voice. "What's up?"

"After all the classes we've taken together, we've become a pretty good team, right?" he asked. "And we're pretty talented?"

"Sure? I mean, we're talented at some things, but not others. Like golf."

"Oh, this definitely isn't golf. I don't think I'll show my face on a golf course any time soon." He chuckled, low and warm.

Grace pushed away from her desk and stood to walk back and forth in her room. What was he getting at? He obviously had something up his sleeve.

The smile in his voice was so infectious that she started to smile too.

"Well, the Summer Sand Festival has a professional sandcastle building contest every year, but they also have an amateur contest. I entered this year's contest a while back under Ariana's name as a promotional thing. It was an impulsive decision at the time, but now I'm left with no one available to help me in the competition," he explained. "I think I'll have better luck if I have someone on my team. Will you help me?"

"Oh. Yeah, of course!" Grace's grin widened.

"Perfect. Can I come pick you up in about ten or so minutes?"

"Sure, I'll be ready!"

They hung up, and Grace changed her clothes into something that was better for building a sandcastle. There was no way she'd escape without getting sand all over the place, so she wore comfortable shorts and a t-shirt that she wouldn't mind getting dirty. Joshua arrived about ten minutes later, also dressed for the occasion, and they headed off toward the beach.

The Summer Sand Festival was in full swing. Grace remembered it in its early days, when it had been just a few booths and a bonfire. Now it was a sprawling event, spreading throughout town and up and down the boardwalk.

"Wow, this is amazing," she said as they passed by a few booths. "I can't believe how many artisans are here."

"Yeah, it's been growing really fast. I haven't taken time to explore it in a few years, except for popping into the food section to taste some things, of course."

"I can smell it from here." Grace tilted her head back and inhaled. It didn't smell like any one food in particular—it just smelled like something delicious that she wanted. Depending on how the contest went, Grace figured they could go get a celebratory treat or something to soothe the loss. Either one would work for her.

Grace followed Joshua down to the beach when they spotted the competition area. They were greeted by an event organizer, who showed them to the spot where a square of sand had been blocked off for them. There was a bag filled with buckets, shovels, spray bottles of water, and other supplies they'd need.

The organizer stepped away, and a few minutes later, a soft horn blew to signal the start of the competition.

"All right!" Grace kneeled on the sand, peering into the bag of supplies. "What's the plan? What do you want to make?"

"That's where I hoped you'd come in. I was going to be ambitious and try to make the building that Ariana is in, but then I remembered I have absolutely *no* building skills and I haven't made a sandcastle since I was about five." Joshua laughed and kneeled down next to her, turning his hat backward and putting his sunglasses on. "What do you think we should do?"

"Hm..." Grace looked around at the other amateur competitors. They were in small groups too. Some were building truly impressive towers and traditional castles, while others were trying to make sea creatures or boats. "It looks like everyone is going sea-themed or classic. Maybe we could try to make something food-related?"

"I think that might be above our pay grade, unless we make a tiered cake." Joshua sat back on his heels. "Or maybe we could just make a bigger and better castle than anyone else."

"Sure, why not?" Grace grabbed a bucket. "Like a grand castle."

"Fit for a queen."

"Or king."

Grace smiled. "Do you want to try to sketch out a plan, or do you want to just see what happens?"

"I think everyone else has a plan, but they seem way more prepared. Let's just see what happens and get creative with it." Joshua grabbed a bucket too. "Maybe we should start with a base of some kind. A big rectangle to put everything else on."

Grace agreed, and they started to build it up. The sand was crumbly, of course, but even when they got it damp, it was difficult to build up a platform with even sides and straight edges.

"Darn it. This seemed so much easier as a child," Joshua muttered, trying to bolster one of the sides.

"I think that was because the sandcastles fell apart right away." Grace patted the side of the base. "Or in my case, I usually ran straight through it after I built it."

Joshua laughed. "So you built a whole sandcastle and destroyed it?"

"Destroying it was the fun part!" She shrugged, setting up her side of the base. "You never built one and destroyed it like a kid Godzilla?"

"Nope. I clearly missed out." Joshua smiled at her, making the dimple in his cheek pop out.

"Maybe we can do that today," Grace said. Then

she crowed in delight. "I got the sides to stay! It needs a little more water on it than you'd think."

Joshua followed her advice and nodded. "Ah. There we go! It looks like... well, like a platform."

"So let's set up the outer walls. Do we want to make it medieval, or something more abstract?" Grace asked, scooping up some sand.

"Let's go abstract."

They worked in tandem, suggesting ideas and creating whatever they wanted, adding in towers and fun shapes until they created something that looked more or less like a castle. It was much more challenging that Grace had thought it would be, but in a good way. They problem-solved together and found solutions to every hurdle they came across.

Grace swept sand off her fingers, though she had the feeling that she was going to be covered in sand for days after this. It was in her hair and stuck all over her skin where it had gotten wet.

"It looks pretty cool." Joshua stood and looked at their piece, tilting his head to the side.

"Does it look better if you turn your head?" Grace asked with a laugh, turning hers too.

After a few failed attempts to build it tall, they had built it wide with a few different layers and tiers.

It was more of an estate than a castle, but it had a unique look that Grace really liked.

"No, it looks about the same. I like it."

"I do too. Hopefully the judges will feel the same way." As she spoke, Grace spotted them coming down the row with clipboards.

Even though she hadn't had this sandcastle contest in mind when she'd woken up that morning, she was happy to be there. She and Joshua really did make a great team. He never tried to bulldoze her ideas and had kept things light with a few jokes.

"Hello," one of the judges said as the small group of officials came up to their castle. "We're here to take a look at what you've done."

"Sure thing." Joshua gently put his hand on Grace's back and guided her out of the way so the judges could look.

She was surprised at how nervous she was, and Joshua seemed to sense it.

"What if one of them trips and falls onto it?" Joshua murmured in her ear.

"Oh, no." Grace snorted. "That would be a little tragic. All of our hard work! But I doubt it would hurt, on the upside."

"True. Plus, I want to be the one to destroy it so I can live out a childhood dream I never knew I had."

They waited quietly as the judges finished perusing their sandcastle, taking down a few notes before heading on to the next team. Grace let out a breath through her nose as the small group of judges stepped away. They were hard to read, so she had no idea whether she and Joshua had done a good job or not. Even though it was just for fun, she always wanted to do her best.

"Well, we did all that we can do," she murmured with a shrug and a smile.

"True." Joshua looked down the line of sandcastles. "At least we won't have to wait long to hear the results. There are only a few more castles to be judged."

They sat down in the sand next to their creation and waited. Grace absently played with some sand, making a dome, and Joshua made one next to hers.

"I think I'm going to wander around the festival after this," she said, packing more sand into the dome she was making.

"Yeah? What part, or have you not decided yet?" he asked.

"I'm not sure. I definitely want to stop by the food part, which probably isn't a surprise to you."

"Nope, not at all. You know that's where I'd want to go too. I know a few restaurant owners who have booths there, if you want recommendations."

"I'd love some! Does Ariana not have a booth?" Grace traced a circle around her mound of sand in a spiral shape. "It's not really 'booth' type food, though, I guess."

"Yeah, it's not. I mean, we could do something small like crostini, but it didn't feel worth the time and effort." Joshua patted down the top of his sand mound before crushing it. "I'd highly recommend the Empanada Abuela booth. I could eat those empanadas every day of the week."

"Oh, their storefront is on the far side of town, right? I've been dying to try it out!"

"It is. The line is usually out the door on a weekend afternoon. You can't go awry with any of the flavors they have."

Joshua told her more about the empanadas and how he'd met the owner, a mother and her adult son whose family always bugged them to make empanadas for family gatherings. Grace's mouth watered as Joshua talked about all the flavors, plus the other restaurants that he knew would be at the festival. Eventually, one of the judges waved everyone over, and the participants gathered.

"Okay, thank you all for participating in this

year's amateur sandcastle contest!" one judge said. "We're excited to announce the winners."

Grace held Joshua's hand as the judges announced the third place winners, a married couple who had lived on the island for decades, the second place winners, a group of high schoolers who were in marching band together, and the first place winners, a group of friends who had built a beautiful sprawling castle that looked almost as amazing as the castles in the professional division.

"Sorry we didn't win," Grace told him after everyone congratulated the winners.

"Hey, at least we had fun," he said with a smile.

He looked at her, and something in his eyes told her that he felt like they really *had* won. Her heart fluttered, and she gently squeezed his hand again.

* * *

"I think I need to grow at least two extra arms," Brooke joked to Hunter, heading back to the bakery's van to gather up more small bags for her treats.

"Do you need a hand?" he asked, turning from his spot manning the bakery's booth at the Summer Sand Festival.

"Nope, I got it. Thanks!" She grabbed the bags

and hustled back to the register that was set up on the long, cloth-covered table. "Turns out two hands work after all."

Her booth at the festival was much different than the one she had put together last year. Now she had a professional banner, branding, and even more treats than ever. Looking back, she was impressed that she'd been able to bake as many things as she had last year without the benefit of the commercial oven at her bakery.

In addition to all of their regular baking, she had stayed late the previous night making everything for the booth. It had been a long night, but Hunter had kept her company after her front counter employee had left for the day. With a little music and plenty to sample, it had been fun instead of an extra chore.

"Would you like to try some of our wild berry muffins?" Brooke asked someone who had slowed down to see what the gathering crowd around the booth was doing.

"Sure!" The woman grabbed a toothpick and poked one of the chunks of muffin that she had cut up. Her eyes widened as she took a bite, nodding. "Wow, that's amazing!"

"Thank you! It's one of our many muffins, if

you'd like to take a look." Brooke grinned before moving on to another customer.

"What would you recommend?" a man pushing a stroller back and forth asked.

"Depends on what you're after." She peered into the stroller, where a toddler was playing with a stuffed tiger. "Is it for this little one?"

"Yes, and for me." The man laughed. "I need a sugar rush, and she *wants* a sugar rush but probably shouldn't have one."

Brooke laughed. "How about one of our chocolate walnut muffins for you and a classic chocolate chip for your little one?"

"That sounds good to me."

She quickly bagged up the man's treats and passed him off to Hunter, who rang him up. She thought she would get a brief reprieve after that, but more and more people kept coming. Seeing their excitement as they tasted their samples boosted her energy, as it always did. Her feet were going to be aching at the end of the day, but it would be worth it to satisfy Marigold's sweet tooth.

"Hey, hun!" Rosa, one of Brooke's regular customers, appeared at the front of the line. She worked in one of the offices nearby the bakery and, like Travis, she brought treats to her coworkers all the time.

"Hey, Rosa!" Brooke said. "It's nice to see you!"

"It's great seeing you too." Rosa waved someone over, a middle-aged man with salt and pepper hair. "This is my husband, Jon. I don't think he's ever come in with me."

"Nice to meet you!" Jon said, shaking Brooke's hand with an enthusiastic grip. "I've been a fan from afar since Rosa brings home those amazing cupcakes of yours all the time. The dark chocolate ones with that creamy filling? They're the best."

"Yes, those are some of my personal favorites too!" Brooke scanned what they had left behind the glass. "We have some if you're interested."

"I'm always interested," he said with a laugh, putting his hand on his stomach. "I'll always make room for dessert."

Brooke put a selection of cupcakes into a box for Rosa and Jon—two of the chocolate and cream, two carrot cake, one lemon, and one red velvet—making more small talk. Knowing that she was part of someone's life the way she was in Rosa's touched her heart. The couple had gone out of their way to find the booth just so that Rosa could introduce her to Jon.

"Here you go," Brooke said, handing over their box plus a little bag with a few madeleines inside. "With a little extra something for being so sweet."

"Thank you!" Rosa took the box. "And you're the sweet one. Literally."

They all chuckled and said their goodbyes. Brooke took a moment to restock some of the cookies that Hunter was selling, spreading them out behind the glass as Hunter took on a new customer.

"Have you tried these white chocolate and roasted macadamia nut cookies?" Hunter asked the young couple who were eyeing the cookies Brooke had just put out. "They're addictive. I can't get enough of them. They're perfect with coffee and a little milk. Want a sample?"

"Sure, why not?" the woman said.

Brooke put out more treats, keeping one eye on the woman as she sampled the cookie.

"Amazing, right?" Hunter said with a charming and genuine smile. "Every time Brooke bakes something I think she can't top it, but then she does. Constantly."

Brooke's cheeks flushed, her heart warming as if she'd just downed some of the coffee Hunter had suggested. Ever since they had met, even when she wasn't sure if she'd even like him as a person, he had been a fan of her baking.

She smiled a little at the memory of going into his home—now their home—with Angela and Lydia, scones in hand, to convince him to stop his efforts to build a big hotel on the island. Even though the conversation hadn't gone the way they'd planned, she remembered the look of wonder on his face as he'd bitten into first one, then *another* of her scones.

"Hi, how can I help you?" Brooke asked, shaking herself out of her thoughts when more customers appeared.

Even as she helped the next customer, her heart beat faster and faster as she saw Hunter continue to upsell her baked goods with all he had. He was enthusiastic about her baking and about her business, and she knew it was more than just his investment in the bakery or his love of her sweets.

It was because he loved *her*.

She loved him too, more than she had ever thought possible. She had been on pins and needles ever since she'd found the ring in his drawer. When was he going to pop the question?

CHAPTER NINETEEN

Grace shut the front door of the inn behind her as she entered, taking in the warm, clean scent of the lobby that made her feel right at home. She had been exploring the island again and had found another spot that had been a favorite of her dad's. It was the perfect place for some photos for the collection she was working on for Nicole's gallery.

Grace waved at Angela, who was on the phone behind the front desk. When she approached, the blonde woman hung up with a blink.

"What's up?" Grace asked, leaning against the desk.

"That was Rachel, of all people," Angela said. "She's in Boston for business and wants to come to Marigold to say hi."

"Wow, really?" Grace hadn't seen the fourth person in their little group of childhood friends in ages. "That's great!"

"I know, right? We're getting the whole gang back together." Angela grinned. "She'll be here in a few hours."

"So soon! I should probably get cleaned up." Grace had worked up a bit of a sweat hiking around and was covered in bug spray and sunscreen.

She headed up to her room and took a shower, then filled the rest of the wait by working on the photos she had just taken. Soon, she got a text from Angela telling her to come down. Grace rushed down the stairs, feeling like she had when they'd all been reunited for the first time over the summer as kids. Lydia was waiting downstairs too, looking just as excited.

The front door cracked open a little bit, and Rachel popped her head in. She broke into a huge grin when she saw her old friends waiting.

"Guys! It's been too long!" Rachel said, opening her arms for the barrage of hugs that came her way.

Grace gave Rachel an extra squeeze before letting her go and looking her over. Rachel looked older, of course, but somehow still the same. She still had strawberry blonde hair, cut just above her shoulders, and her blue eyes were still friendly and warm. Freckles were sprinkled across her cheeks, a little darker now that it was summer.

Rachel's eyes widened as she looked up at the inn's lobby, taking in all of the changes. Grace had to smile. She'd had the same awed reaction when she had seen the inn again.

"This place looks so beautiful, you guys," Rachel breathed, putting her hand to her chest. "You did such an amazing job. It's like it used to be, but better, if that makes sense."

"Thank you!" Angela said. "That was our goal."

"Let me get a picture of all of you guys," Kathy said, peering around the corner from the office, her camera in hand.

The four women gathered together at the front desk, looping their arms around each other and grinning widely as Kathy took a few quick snapshots.

"Perfect!" Kathy examined the photos in the viewfinder. "I'll get these on my computer and send them around. I think it would be really sweet on Instagram. A reunion at the Beachside Inn."

"That's a great idea!" Lydia said. "I'll see if I can find an old photo of the four of us to put with it."

"Oh no, hopefully one from a summer where I didn't have those horrendous bangs." Rachel snorted.

"All of us had terrible bangs at one point or another, so finding a picture where all of us have perfect hair will probably be a struggle." Angela chuckled. "Do you remember the time I gave myself highlights? Ugh, what was I thinking?"

"Those *were* pretty terrible." Rachel's smile made her eyes twinkle, just as they had so often when they were teenagers. "But we're to blame too since we encouraged you. Then again, we all enabled each other's poor hair choices."

"Seriously. At least we got it out of our systems back then," Lydia said. Then she clapped her hands together. "Let's talk more over some food. I'm hungry."

They all said goodbye to Kathy and headed out to a great bistro that Grace had stumbled upon during one of her walks around town a little while back. It had great views of the harbor, and with the sun streaming in through the windows, brightening up the white walls and wood floors, Grace's mood lifted even higher than before.

"Cheers to reunions," Rachel declared, holding up her glass of wine.

"Cheers!"

The old friends clinked their glasses together and took a sip. Marigold had seriously spoiled Grace with good wine. Every single wine she'd tasted was delicious and refreshing, even the kinds that she had previously written off. The food was just as good, of course.

Angela recommended a few menu items, and just like in the old days, they got a few dishes to split—a summery couscous salad, gazpacho, fresh shrimp in an herby sauce, the fresh catch of the day, and a selection of homemade breads. It was a far cry from the pizzas loaded with ten toppings, cookies, sodas, and fries that they used to share.

"So, how are things in Chicago?" Lydia asked Rachel. "How's life in general?"

"There's so much to catch up on," Rachel said with a smile. "But things are great! I love Chicago, even though the winters are pretty terrible. My daughter Sierra is already eight, which is crazy to think about, and my husband Doug loves his career as an architect. There's always something under construction there, so he hasn't run low on projects."

"Yeah, I bet!" Angela smiled. "And wow, Sierra's eight? Jake is just a little younger than her."

"It's a great age." Rachel nodded. "But it's a little terrifying because it feels like she's growing up so fast."

"I know that feeling." Lydia snagged a piece of

bread and tore it in half, spreading some butter onto it. "I swear, sometimes I look at Holly and wonder when she went from the little girl who was afraid of monsters under her bed to a grown woman half-way through her college degree."

"Wow." Rachel laughed. "College? Already?"

"Trust me, I feel old every time I think about it."

The women caught each other up on their lives as they enjoyed their meal, chatting about everything from the last time they had all been together to college to their relationships. Their paths had initially started the way that everyone expected them to. They'd gone to college and started solid careers. But Grace's path had veered off when her father had gotten sick, as had Lydia's when Paul had passed away. Rachel had experienced some bumps in her career, and Angela had gone through her divorce.

But after it all, they had ended up here, happily talking about the positives in their lives. There were so many to share.

"I'm so excited for all of you. You've each done such amazing things—not that I ever doubted you'd do anything less," Rachel said, topping off everyone's glasses of wine. "And I'm really proud of you for coming back here to reset, Grace."

"Thank you." Grace raised her glass to Rachel

and took a sip. "It's been amazing to come back. I feel better than I have in years."

"Maybe it was meant to be, just like this little reunion." Rachel swirled her wine around in her glass. "Like your path was supposed to loop back around and settle here for good."

"Maybe so." Grace took a few moments to serve herself a little bit more of the fish of the day. It was light, flaky, and buttery, almost melting in her mouth with every bite. "The thought of staying is really appealing, especially with Joshua here."

"Yeah?" Angela tilted her head to the side, her eyebrows lifting slightly. They had discussed Grace staying long-term in the past, but Grace had never outright said that she was seriously considering it.

"Yeah." Grace held back a smile, looking down at her plate. "I have real feelings for him. I didn't even mean for it to happen—I even tried to make it *not* happen—but here I am. I've never felt like this about a man. For real this time, as often as I know I said that in high school."

They all laughed.

"Stay and see how it all comes together," Lydia said.

"Yeah, seriously. It's definitely worth a shot," Angela added. "Remember that travel blogger,

Meredith Walters, who's getting married at the inn in the fall? You could do her wedding photography. And anyone else who gets married at the inn."

"That's a great idea! We can refer you when they book the space or include you as a part of it," Lydia says, whipping out her phone. "I'm just taking a few notes so I don't forget this."

"That really is a great idea," Grace said, thinking about the wedding photos she had in her portfolio.

She thought about her future—her photography at the inn and in the gallery, her friends, Joshua. It all felt like it was truly possible.

They wrapped up the meal with a delicious carrot cake and headed back to the inn, their stomachs stuffed. They stood on the porch as if they didn't want the evening to end.

"This has been amazing, guys," Rachel said. "I wish I could stay longer, but I have this plane to catch.

"It has. I wish you could stay longer, too." Grace squeezed Rachel's shoulder.

The women gave Rachel hugs, vowing to have another reunion soon, and saw her off. Grace felt herself tear up a little bit, but she mostly savored the warm, happy feeling that was filling her body from head to toe.

* * *

"Hey, you," Lydia said as she let herself into Grant's house.

He had given her a key a while back and was expecting her, so he was waiting by the back door that led into his kitchen, a bottle of wine in hand. As always, her heart lit up when she saw him. They'd both had busy weeks and they hadn't had the chance to see each other as much as they liked to.

"Hi there." Grant gave her a peck on the lips. "How was dinner?"

"It was great! It was so nice catching up with Rachel and hearing all about her life in Chicago." She tapped the top of the wine bottle. "Want to have a glass and talk about it?"

"Of course. Go get settled. The fireplace should be going by now." He gave her another kiss, on the cheek this time, and Lydia did as he said.

She poked at the fire a little bit, making it burn a little brighter. Since it was summer, the fire was more for ambience than warmth, so she didn't mess with it more. She curled up on the couch, accepting a glass of merlot from Grant when he came in. They fell into position as they always did—Grant's arm went around her and Lydia curled up against his side.

She sipped her wine, feeling even more content and happy than ever. Grant's soft t-shirt smelled like him in the best way—a mix of fresh grass and laundry.

"We were talking to Grace about possibly doing photos for Meredith Walters' wedding in the fall," Lydia said against his t-shirt.

"Yeah? That sounds like a perfect fit."

"I know! It got me thinking, too. What if we get married at the inn too? Just something small, nothing extravagant." Lydia looked up at him with a smile. "It'll be a way of celebrating what brought us together. I think it would be very 'us.'"

Grant smiled, the smile lines around his eyes getting a little deeper. "I love that. Let's do it."

He gave her another kiss, and she could feel the curve of his lips as they both kept smiling.

CHAPTER TWENTY

Brooke had been running around the bakery all day, half-covered in flour. She juggled customers, extra batches of cookies, calls from her suppliers, and more with what she hoped was grace. It felt like things were going well, at least. She had gotten a huge rush in the store after the booth at the Summer Sand Festival, both locals and tourists stopping by for more treats. The line had been out the door for most of the morning.

She flopped down on a stool in the back and guzzled half of her water bottle in one go. Finally, things were quiet. She had flipped the "open" sign to "closed," and Gretchen, the girl who worked the front counter, had left for the day.

Brooke wondered if she should do what Lydia

and Angela had done and hire more help soon. Kathy had seriously helped them not go nuts from all the pressures of being business owners. Gretchen was great and very reliable, but she was only one person. Brooke debated what kind of help to get, momentarily feeling overwhelmed before taking a moment to appreciate that this was a good problem to have. She had customers every day, many of them loyal.

She yawned and finished off her water, pushing to her feet to finish closing up for the day, wiping everything down, sweeping up crumbs, and making sure that the doughs that needed to be prepared the night before were done. Once she locked the door behind her, she picked up a few things from the grocery store and the pet store before heading home.

She took the long route on her favorite back roads to give herself more time to think. For whatever reason, her car was the perfect spot for her to work things out. It was quiet, and she couldn't get swept up in one of the many distractions on her phone. Her brain could drift to whatever pushed its way to the front of her mind. She wanted her bakery to be as beloved as The Sweet Creamery someday and she couldn't do that without more help.

There was so much she could accomplish. Maybe someday there would be another location, or maybe some of their more popular treats could be sold in grocery stores or online. If the owners of the Sweet Creamery got on board, she would love to make a collaboration flavor with some of her cookies or brownies mixed into one of their ice creams. Most of her friends and family did that on their own, topping a brownie with some ice cream, so it felt like a natural fit.

The field where she had once driven past Hunter on her way home from taking Scratch to the vet was up ahead. Every time she passed it, she had to smile. She had genuinely thought he was hurt, not rehearsing for an audition. He had been so into his work that he hadn't realized just how convincing he would be to any passerby.

The sun had just set, but it wasn't pitch black yet, making the sky a rich, beautiful deep blue. It blended in with the ocean at the horizon, the only illumination coming from beautiful lights set up on the beach. Her brow furrowed as she spotted Hunter on the beach, kneeling down and doing something she couldn't see. *Now* was he hurt? He liked this spot of the beach too, but he rarely hung out here this late without her.

Brooke slowed to a stop and got out of her car, rushing toward him.

"Hunter?" she called out, her heart pounding hard and fast. "Are you okay?"

Once she got close to the beach, she froze. The lights weren't just scattered across the sand in random places as she had thought at first. Instead, they were set out in a very particular arrangement, spelling out a few words.

Will you marry me?

Brooke blinked, looking between Hunter and the lights for a few moments, her mind momentarily going blank. Her heart was still racing so quickly that it was all she could hear. Hunter smiled, taking her hand for a moment before getting down on one knee.

"Will you marry me, Brooke? Will you make me the luckiest man in the world?" he asked, looking up at her. Then he opened the little velvet box, revealing a gorgeous ring.

Brooke's hand flew up to her mouth, a gasp falling from her lips.

* * *

Hunter looked up at the woman he loved, whose blue eyes were round with shock. The hand covering her mouth was trembling, and he felt his hands holding the box doing the same. He thought he had been more nervous than he'd ever been in his life when he had asked Brooke's parents for their blessing, but this was a whole new level of anxiety he'd never felt before. It felt as if an entire eon passed as he waited for her answer, which would change the course of his life.

She gazed down at him for a long moment, tears in her eyes, then gave him a shaky smile.

"Yes, yes, yes!" she exclaimed.

If Hunter hadn't been kneeling already, he would have collapsed with relief. He slid the ring onto her finger, a perfect fit, and got to his feet, kissing her with all he had. His world finally felt complete. He gave her a few more brief kisses, pulling her even closer into his arms and burying his face in her hair. She always smelled sweet, and knowing he'd get to hold her like this for the rest of his life almost made her smell sweeter.

They finally pulled apart, and Brooke wiped the tears from her eyes, a small smile making her lips quirk up.

"I have a little secret," she said, looking at the ground, then up at him through her lashes. "I... I found the ring a little while ago by accident."

"Really?" Hunter's eyes widened. "I thought I was being so sneaky."

They both laughed, still holding each other.

"If I hadn't been half-asleep and getting dressed in the dark, I probably wouldn't have found it. I've been going crazy wondering if or when you were going to do it. This was perfect. I'm still shaking a little from the surprise of it all."

Hunter kissed her forehead and squeezed her waist. "There's more, actually."

"More? How can you make this moment better than it already is?"

He stepped back and gestured to a blanket he'd set out a few feet away from the lights. "I thought we could have a little nighttime beach picnic to celebrate."

Brooke's face lit up even more and she gave him another kiss. He loved seeing her face like that, her blue eyes sparkling even in the low light.

"Let's eat," he said, taking her by the hand and guiding her to the blanket.

"Wow, what did you pack?" Brooke asked. "I don't think we've ever had a picnic together before."

"I got a bunch of different things. I had a little help, admittedly." He smiled and sat down on the blanket, unpacking the basket. "There's that roasted chicken salad you like, plus some baguettes to eat it on. And these homemade chips—both regular and sweet potato mixed together. And some fruit and smaller things."

Brooke clapped her hands together, then grabbed the chips. "It's perfect! All of my favorite picnic foods. I'm guessing my parents helped?"

"Yeah. I called them to ask for their blessing, and they were excited. When I ran the idea of a proposal here by them, your mom suggested a picnic." He grabbed the plates and silverware he'd packed. "Oh, and there's champagne, of course."

"This is definitely a champagne moment." Brooke leaned forward and kissed him again, giggling as if she couldn't help herself. Hunter loved it—he loved everything about her. "Let's pop it and celebrate."

CHAPTER TWENTY-ONE

Travis pushed the door to his parents' house open, the noise and smells of delicious food washing over him. As was often the case, he and Jennifer were the last ones to arrive, showing up with a great bottle of wine in hand. It had been a long day at the station for him, and Jennifer's day had been packed full of appointments to show homes, so they were both excited to unwind.

"Hi, Travis! Hi, Jennifer!" Jake exclaimed, skidding across the hardwood in his socks. His hair was sticking up in every direction, almost as if electricity were coursing through him.

"Hey, Jake!" Travis gave his nephew their customary high-five. "You're back from your dad's?"

"Yup!" Jake gave Jennifer a high-five too and

darted off again, leaving Jennifer and Travis laughing.

"How can kids have so much energy?" she asked, walking toward the kitchen.

"I don't know. Honestly, I'm jealous. I wish I could bottle that up." Travis followed her, happy to see how comfortably his girlfriend moved around the house now. She didn't wait for him to guide her or stick close to his side as she had the first time or two that she'd come over.

Jennifer had taken to his family quickly, already getting close to all of them. He was thrilled. He couldn't have asked for more when it came to their relationship. One of the biggest takeaways he had from his failed online dating days was that family really mattered to him, and anyone he dated had to get along with his family and understand just how important they were in his life.

"How are you guys?" Travis asked as he stepped into the epicenter of the house's chaos, the kitchen.

"Good! Help us bring the food out, would you?" Phoebe asked, crossing the kitchen with a big platter of baked chicken.

Travis and Jennifer pitched in, with Jennifer helping Angela set the table and Travis helping Phoebe carry out the bigger platters. Soon the table was covered with dishes that would have made anyone's mouth water. In addition to the baked chicken, there were fresh vegetables from Phoebe's garden, lentil salad, regular salad, fragrant, fluffy rice, and a few things Travis couldn't even recognize. Whatever it was, he was going to try it. He'd eaten a light lunch in preparation.

They settled around the table, Travis sitting between Phoebe and Jennifer. Everyone passed around dishes, starting to fill up their plates as Mitch went around and served some wine.

"Before you guys dig in, I wanted to make a toast in honor of Brooke and Hunter's engagement," Mitch said, standing at the head of the table. "We're excited to have you in the family for good, Hunter."

"To Brooke and Hunter!" Phoebe added, raising her glass.

Everyone followed suit with a few murmurs of "hear, hear." The clinking of glasses filled the room, and there were smiles all around.

Travis had been worried when Brooke and Hunter had first started dating. There Hunter was, fresh out of Hollywood and extremely charming, and Travis hadn't been sure he could trust him to treat Brooke well. Now he felt a bit silly for even thinking that. Hunter was a kind, genuine person and didn't have an ounce of the ego that one would expect from a big movie star—he was exactly the kind of man Travis was happy to have as his future brother in law.

"Okay, now you all can eat," Mitch said, sitting down and gesturing for everyone to dig in.

The room erupted into chatter as people dug in and added more to their plates.

"Can you hand me that quinoa, hun?" Phoebe asked Travis. He nodded and passed her the dish.

"Since when were you a quinoa person, Mom?"

"Ever since I tried this recipe that makes it taste like something delicious and not the unpleasant cousin of couscous." Phoebe put some on her plate and handed the dish back to Travis, taking the opportunity to lean a little closer to him. "Maybe someday we'll be celebrating you and Jennifer at one of these dinners."

Travis nodded and picked up his fork again, a grin tugging at his lips. The thought of marrying Jennifer didn't make him feel nervous or skittish at all. He had waited a long time for the right person, and she had been worth the wait. There wasn't anything to be anxious about.

He glanced over at the beautiful blonde realtor as he speared a potato on his fork and found her watching him, one eyebrow up. In the time they had been together, he'd gotten good at deciphering what those looks of hers meant. This one seemed to be asking about the same thing Travis had just been thinking about—was Phoebe's hint going to make him skittish?

Instead of answering with words, Travis just smiled and leaned over to give her a quick kiss. When he pulled back, she was smiling too.

* * *

Lydia laid in bed, staring at the ceiling. Her stomach was pleasantly full after the lovely dinner she'd had with Grant, Holly, and Nicolas while Angela was at her weekly family dinner. She'd had a glass or two of wine as well, which usually put her right to sleep, but she couldn't drift off despite the late hour.

No use in tossing and turning, she thought, stepping out of bed and into her slippers. She headed downstairs, hearing some quiet sounds in the living room. As she got closer, she realized the TV was on in the living room. Holly was curled up on the couch watching some late night talk show.

Lydia smiled and walked past her, heading into the kitchen. Inside, there was a pint of the Sweet Creamery's Mega Chocolate ice cream—a white chocolate ice cream with a ribbon of dark chocolate syrup, bits of brownie, and crunchy candies. It was a new flavor, and both Lydia and Holly had fallen in love with it instantly.

"Late night ice cream?" Lydia asked, making her way back into the living room with the pint and two spoons.

"Ooh! Yeah, of course." Holly perked up. "I forgot that was in the freezer."

"I could never forget about it." Lydia sat down on the couch and opened the pint, holding it between the two of them. "I never thought white chocolate ice cream would taste good, but it's so delicious."

"It really is." Holly turned off the TV, leaving the faint glow from the lamp as the only light source in the room.

The two of them dug in together, easily downing a quarter of the pint before coming up for air.

"You couldn't sleep either?" Lydia asked.

Holly shook her head, digging around for a brownie chunk. "Nah. I've just been thinking, and I couldn't drift off."

"What's on your mind?"

Holly took a bite of ice cream, sucking on the spoon for a moment as she gathered her thoughts.

"How did you know that Dad was the right one? And Grant?"

Lydia shrugged. "It's just a feeling, honestly. It's about how you feel when you're with them, and how they support you through thick and thin. I know that's kind of vague, but that's all I can say. Why?"

Holly nodded, scooping up a small bite. "Nic and I have been talking about marriage a little bit."

Lydia was proud of herself for not choking on a brownie bite in surprise or flying into overprotective mom mode right away. The more she thought about it, the less surprised she got. They were clearly in love with each other, and were willing to stick through the bumps in the road to stay close to each other.

But they were so young. There were so many things that were ahead of them, things they couldn't anticipate. Still, maybe they could roll with the punches together instead of floundering on their own.

"That's a big step," Lydia said quietly, careful to keep her tone neutral.

"You're freaking out, aren't you?" Holly grinned, polishing off the last bite of ice cream.

"A little. You know me." Lydia chuckled. "But I

like Nicolas a lot, and I like you two together. Just remember that there's no rush."

"I know." Holly smiled and put the empty pint down on the coffee table. "Thanks, Mom."

She gave Lydia a hug, squeezing her tight. Lydia held on to her daughter for an extra moment before letting go.

"Want to watch a cheesy Hallmark movie?" Holly asked after looking at the clock behind Lydia. "A new one should be starting in a minute or two."

"Sure, why not?"

Lydia grabbed a throw blanket and put it over them both, settling in for some late night fun.

CHAPTER TWENTY-TWO

The restaurant's office felt even smaller than usual with both Alan and their sous chef Connor inside it, but Joshua didn't mind. He was just excited to make more progress on the ideas that he and Alan had been batting back and forth. Once they'd gotten the ball rolling, ideas had sprung up left and right. So far, they had decided that they wanted the restaurant to be more of a cousin to Ariana rather than a sibling. All of the menu ideas that Alan had come up with were great starts, and they'd collaborated well on a few other ideas that needed some tweaking.

Connor wasn't in the loop yet, and Joshua could see the confusion written all over the sous chef's face at having a meeting in the office instead of the kitchen. He had worked for

Joshua for several years and had always done great work, so he really had nothing to worry about.

"Take a breath, Connor," Joshua reassured him, opening up his laptop on his desk. "This is going to be fun."

"Fun?" Connor's eyebrow went up, his youthful face scrunching up a little with confusion.

"Seriously. And not 'oh, we just got a last minute party and all of them want changes to their dishes' fun," Alan added with a chuckle, pulling up his chair closer to Joshua's desk.

Connor laughed. "Okay, so real fun, not masochistic fun. What's going on?"

"You probably know that I've been playing with the idea of opening a restaurant in Boston, right?" Joshua asked. Connor nodded, his brown hair glinting in the light. "Well, Alan and I have been talking about it and decided to go in a slightly different direction. Alan's going to partner with me and head to Boston to open the new restaurant in my stead, which means that we'd like to promote you to head chef here."

"What? Seriously?" Connor looked between the two of them, his eyes lighting up. "Me?"

"Of course, you. Who else?" Alan laughed.

"You've done amazing work and you can handle the kitchen just like I would."

"Wow...." Connor looked to Joshua. "Does this mean you'll be here in Marigold for good?"

"Yup," Joshua confirmed. "I'll be in charge of this location and head to Boston on a day trip every once in a while to see how things are doing."

"Wow," Connor murmured again, sitting back in his chair with a big grin on his face. "So we'd work together on the specials and everything?"

"Of course. You've had great ideas in the past, so I'm sure we'll come up with some great things," Joshua said.

"This is an honor, really. I'd love to be head chef."

"Perfect!" Joshua grinned too, extending his hand to Connor so they could shake on it. The younger man gave his hand an enthusiastic shake, then shook Alan's hand too. "I think this deserves a toast."

"I'll get some glasses." Alan stood up. "What kind?"

"Some whiskey glasses. I have something hidden away here."

Joshua went to the tiny closet in his office and unearthed a bottle of good whiskey he'd been saving for the right occasion. This was definitely the time to open it. Now his plans felt even more real and more exciting than ever. He would be able to grow his business, see Alan and Connor's careers transform, and share more good food with more people.

And most importantly, he could finally put down roots. No more running himself into the ground to hit a goal, only to move the finish line back immediately after achieving it.

Alan returned to the office with three glasses, and Joshua filled each one with a little whiskey.

"To new chapters?" Connor said, picking it up and raising it.

"To new chapters."

The three men clinked their glasses together and sipped the whiskey, which went down smooth, warming Joshua's chest. It really was a new chapter of his life, one he was excited to turn the page to.

* * *

"Hey, Jennifer! Thanks for meeting me here," Grace said as she walked up to the friendly real estate agent in downtown Marigold.

"No problem at all! I'm excited to show you around a little bit." Jennifer smiled. "I've found some amazing places that should fit your needs. A few are near the water, and so many of them have amazing views."

"I'm excited too!" Grace had woken up much earlier than normal, so filled with anticipation that she couldn't drift back off to sleep.

"Let's go, then. The first apartment is just two blocks away, which means there's a ton of easy access to all these great little shops." Jennifer gestured to her right and Grace followed her.

The location was already a massive check in the "pro" column, and they hadn't even gotten inside yet. It was close to the grocery store and pharmacy, plus several of the fast-casual restaurants that Grace had come to love in her time here.

Jennifer unlocked the door to the first apartment building, which was nice and relatively new. It didn't quite have the charm that Grace was looking for, at least on the outside, but she was open to seeing more.

"This apartment is a one bedroom, but there's tons of space and a gorgeous bath." Jennifer led them both up the stairs and to the end of the hall.

Grace walked inside the apartment first, taking it all in. It was lovely, with just enough space for the furniture she wanted to keep from her home in Colorado and a nice view beyond some trees.

Jennifer let Grace poke around, opening the cabinets to see how much space there was for all of her cooking supplies and seeing how much closet space there was. Everything had been painted muted colors for the sake of showing the space, but Grace could imagine putting her own touch around the place. But still, something was missing that she couldn't put her finger on.

"So, what do you think? Do you have any questions?" Jennifer asked once Grace came out of the bedroom and back into the living room.

"I think it's nice! It definitely has everything I was looking for, more or less." Grace took another look around. "But it doesn't quite feel like a perfect fit, at least not yet."

"No problem. Let's go look at our next place." Jennifer opened the door for her, and they headed back down to the street.

The next apartment was easy to get to on foot, yet another bonus of living in downtown Marigold. Jennifer and Grace put on their sunglasses, the midday sun beating down on them.

"This place has an even better view," Jennifer said. "Definitely photo-worthy."

"That sounds amazing. I'd love to be able to just take a few steps outside and have perfect photo-ops."

Grace looked around as the gentle bustle of downtown calmed a little bit and the beach came into view. "Is it an ocean view?"

"Yup! You can be on the beach in about four minutes." Jennifer made a right, and soon they were at the building.

It was a large, New England style duplex, split into two apartments. There was a beautiful but small front and back yard, trimmed with blooming flowers. It was much more private than the other apartment, and it had the charm that Grace was looking for. The rent was also way below her budget, which made her chest fill with hope. A beach view, under her budget? It was almost too good to be true.

"Here we are. Your neighbor is the person who owns the building, so they'll be right there in case you need anything." Jennifer opened the door, letting Grace wander inside as she had at the last location.

Right away, Grace felt a little deflated. It really was too good to be true.

The views out of the back window were beautiful, but the inside wasn't. The layout felt a little bit closed in, with walls blocking off the living room from the kitchen, something that Grace wasn't a fan of. The master bedroom was teeny and the closet didn't have much space. For whatever reason, you had to walk through the kitchen to get to the half bath, a design flaw that puzzled her so much that she had to laugh.

"Not a fan?" Jennifer asked with a gentle smile.

"I'm sorry. I hope I'm not pouting!" Grace ran her hand over the ancient Formica countertop. "I'm grateful for your help."

"Don't worry about it. You're going to be the one living here." Jennifer laughed. "The location is one of the most important pieces, so I thought it would be worth showing you."

"Oh, the location is fantastic. But I don't know how I'd feel cooking here with a bathroom just a few feet away." Grace laughed. "On to the next place?"

"Yes, let's head out."

Since it was a nice day, they took a twenty-minute walk to the last place that Jennifer had picked out. The path ran right along the beach, then inland a little bit to a duplex similar to the one that they had just visited. It was on a slight hill, raising it above the grasses and dunes that were a short walk away.

"This one doesn't have a bathroom that opens directly into a kitchen." Jennifer grinned as she got the key out and unlocked the door. "And I have to say that these views are my favorite."

Grace gasped when she got a good look at the apartment for the first time. It had an open floor plan, with beautiful hardwood floors and an abundance of windows, showing off a view of the water and foliage. The kitchen was open to the living room so she could talk to guests as she cooked, and there was a small island, which was more than enough space for her.

She didn't have much of a green thumb, but now that she knew a little bit more about plants from her nature classes, she figured that she'd enjoy dipping her toes into gardening in the small backyard. It was fenced in, too.

"The light in the evening is absolutely gorgeous and you'll be able to see the sunset from your kitchen window," Jennifer told her.

Grace could easily imagine it—sipping a glass of wine while stirring a sauce, looking out onto a golden sunset over the water. She could imagine herself in there in general as she explored the rest of the apartment. It was a tiny bit smaller than the others in terms of square footage, but it felt larger because everything was so airy and light.

The bedroom also had an incredible view of

some grasses and trees off in the distance, and would likely get some of that same beautiful evening light that the kitchen got. Grace didn't have a lot of clothes, but she appreciated the amount of closet space there was. To make it even more perfect, the owners had renovated the bathrooms so there was a huge clawfoot tub, too.

If she had to find any flaw in the place, it was that it was slightly farther from downtown than she initially anticipated, though she was still close to a part of town that had a great grocery store and a few restaurants. The rent was a little higher here than at the other two places, but it was perfect in every other way.

"This is the place. I think this is it," Grace said, coming out of the bedroom. "I absolutely love it."

"Wonderful! I hoped you would." Jennifer clapped her hands together. "Do you want to start on the paperwork today?"

Grace paused and bit her lip, taking another look out the window. She hadn't spoken to Joshua about this yet. What if she had misread things between them? There was a chance he wanted to stay casual. And maybe his feelings for her had faded since the last time they had seen each other.

But even if she didn't have Joshua, she felt like

this apartment would be a perfect home for her. She had her old friends and so many new ones. Her photography business had a lot of promise too, especially with Lydia and Angela's idea to have her do wedding photos at the inn. And it just felt right to her. In the short time she had stayed on the island, it had become home again.

This was where she was meant to be.

"Yes," Grace said with a smile. "Let's start on that paperwork."

CHAPTER TWENTY-THREE

Grace wandered around her room at the inn, trying to mentally put together her to-do list. She had signed her lease on the beautiful beachside apartment Jennifer had shown her, and it was starting soon, so she had a lot of things to do for the move. Plus, she was drumming up more customers for her photography business. The money she'd inherited from her father would keep her afloat for a long while, but she was itching to work with people again as soon as she could.

And another thing on her to-do list: talking with Joshua. Even though she hadn't decided to stay just for his sake, he was certainly a part of why she was staying. In the short time they'd known each other, he had helped her feel rejuvenated and excited about each day.

She dug out her cell phone and called him, and he answered on the second ring.

"Hey, Grace," he said, a smile in his voice. "How are you?"

"I'm great! I was just calling to see if you wanted to meet up today, if you're free." She crossed her fingers, praying he was. She thought she would lose her nerve if she had to wait to tell him for another day.

"Yeah, definitely. Just tell me when and where." The excitement in his voice made Grace smile, too.

"How about we meet downtown at the roundabout. The one that's a block away from the butcher? Maybe around one o'clock?" Grace asked. "It's a nice, central location so we can figure out what we want to do there on the fly."

"Sounds perfect to me. See you then."

Grace had enough time to get ready and do a bit of organizing before she headed into town. She found Joshua standing outside of a small boutique that specialized in swimwear, his hands in the pockets of his jeans as he looked over the display in the window.

Her heart jumped even more than it usually did

when she saw him. If she had passed him on the street without knowing him, she would have noticed how handsome he was no matter how busy it was around him. And knowing that he was a great person made him even more attractive.

"Looking for something?" Grace asked as she approached.

"Hm?" Joshua looked up, a smile on his face. "Well, maybe. I haven't gone clothes shopping in a while. I didn't even know this little place was here."

"It's nice. I got this dress from here, actually." She held out the skirt of her casual linen dress. "And from what I saw, the men's clothing was just as nice."

"I'll have to check it out, then," he said. "What do you want to do while we're here?"

"How about we grab something to nibble on while we walk? It's so gorgeous out that it would be a shame to sit inside." Grace looked around. "I don't know where to start—there's so much good food around here."

"How about some..." Joshua looked around too. "Well, we can't go wrong with ice cream, can we?"

"Definitely not, especially when it's this warm. Let's do it."

They walked down the block toward the Sweet

Creamery and hopped in line, which was spilling a little bit outside.

"Looks like everyone else had the same idea," Joshua said with a smile, stepping aside to let a child with a huge waffle cone filled with rainbow-colored ice cream out of the shop.

"It's a pretty good one." Grace eyed the menu up on the wall, visible from through the window. "I have no idea what to get, though. What are you thinking?"

Joshua looked at the menu too, cocking his head to the side. "A scoop of lavender honey and a scoop of French vanilla sounds like my speed today."

"Final answer?"

"Yup." He grinned. "I've learned to go with my first gut instinct when it comes to picking food. Otherwise I'll end up in analysis paralysis."

"That's a smart call. I'm already there. There are so many flavors to choose from." Grace rested a hand on her hip. "But I'm leaning toward some child-like flavors—something sweet and colorful. Or maybe something chocolate…"

"What was your first impulse when you wanted ice cream?" he asked.

"I wanted something with texture. I love crunchy stuff in my ice cream." Grace looked over at Joshua.

"If you had to pick one for me, your first gut instinct, what would you choose?"

Joshua looked at the menu for a few moments. "I'll keep you in suspense until I order."

"No fair!" Grace said, playfully smacking his arm.

"Hey, you asked for my first instinct. My first one was to surprise you." He shrugged. "It'll be great, I promise."

"Okay, true. You can't really go wrong with a chef and restaurateur picking a flavor combo for you." Grace smiled.

The line moved pretty quickly, and soon they were at the front.

"I'll have a scoop of lavender honey and a scoop of vanilla in a cup, and she'll have a scoop of white chocolate macadamia nut and a scoop of dark chocolate with pretzels on top," Joshua said to the person behind the counter.

"Ooh, that sounds amazing," Grace said, beaming. "I should get you to pick my ice cream pairings all the time."

Joshua laughed. They paid for their ice cream and headed outside toward the boardwalk. Grace took her first bite of the white chocolate macadamia nut, which tasted just as good as the cookie, and then the dark chocolate, then both of them together.

"This is *incredible*," she said, stopping so she could appreciate just how delicious it was. "I was going to go with just chocolate and strawberry with some toasted almonds but this? This is a masterpiece."

"I'm glad you love it. The white chocolate macadamia nut ice cream was too intriguing to pass up even though it's not what I want right now." Joshua kept walking, and Grace fell in step next to him. "Working with chocolate is a skill that I haven't mastered in the slightest."

"Really? Why? Are you not a chocolate person?"

"Oh, I'm very much a chocolate person." He paused to take another bite of his ice cream as they stepped onto the boardwalk. "But chocolate is super finicky to work with. I can do flourless chocolate cake and a ganache, but that's as far as I'll go. Not that I make desserts regularly, but still."

"Well, you have an amazing pastry chef at your disposal."

"That too." His smile made the little lines in the corners of his eyes deepen. "But there's a reason why I went with savory cooking. Once when I was experimenting in my kitchen, just goofing off and trying to make some elaborate candies, I nearly caught my hair on fire."

Grace snorted. "How is that possible?"

"I can't even remember. But it's far from the last time I nearly burned off all my hair."

She scooped up a bit of white chocolate and dark chocolate ice cream, smiling to herself. She liked Joshua's hair, the gray coming in at the temples and the slight cowlick he had on one side of his head when he ran his fingers through it a lot. Her cheeks flushed, thinking about what she had truly asked him out to discuss.

Talking to him was so easy that she knew she could dance around the subject all afternoon without any trouble. But that was only kicking the can down the road. She hadn't come to Marigold to shy away from change, even though it was scary.

"Want to sit down for a second? The view here is nice," Grace said, trying to keep her voice light.

"Sure. It'll be easier to eat this way too."

They both sat down on a bench, which overlooked the beach. Aside from the occasional group of friends or jogger, the view was uninterrupted. Since it was peak busy season, there were clusters of people everywhere, their brightly-colored umbrellas peppering the sand. Some kids were flying kites to Grace's left, and a spirited volleyball game was to her right.

But despite the activity, the sea held her attention. It was bright blue, the sun sparkling off of it. She tried her best to sync her breaths with the tides, just to calm her down. It gave her just enough courage to speak.

"I need to tell you something," they both said at the same time, turning to each other. Then they burst out laughing.

"Apparently we're on the same wavelength," Grace said. "You go first."

"No, you can go. Seriously."

She smiled, looking down into her now empty cup, and took another deep breath.

"I'm staying in Marigold. I just signed a lease at a nice little apartment," she told him.

"Hey, that's great news!" He gently nudged her shoulder. "Congrats."

"Thanks." She swallowed, mustering up just a little more courage to put herself out there. "It's been the best decision I've made for myself in a long, long time. I never thought life would lead me back to the place where I grew up, but here I am."

"This place suits you," he murmured, letting his spoon rest in his cup.

"I agree." She smiled despite her nerves. "When I started taking all the classes with you, I realized just how much life has to offer that I haven't even gotten the chance to explore. Well, and it's shown me what I'm *not* great at."

"Golf?" The corner of his mouth quirked up.

"Definitely golf. It was a nice little trip down memory lane, but I think the thrill of it was bigger when I was a kid, just hanging out with my dad and driving the little cart around." Grace absently poked around in her ice cream. "But you made it fun."

"You made it fun too. Same with every other class we took. I doubt I would have won Alan's bet if you weren't there."

"What did you win?" Grace asked.

Joshua took a bite of his ice cream, looking up at the sky. "Well, nothing tangible. But I think that was what Alan was going for, the sneak. I got to meet you and learn a lot about myself."

"I've learned a lot about myself too. And what I want in life." Grace felt her hands sweating, but she pushed on. "I was thinking that, for as long as you're here in Marigold, I'd like to spend more time with you. Romantically, I mean. I have pretty strong feelings for you. It's been a long time since I've met anyone who I feel so in sync with. Meeting you has been one of the best things that's happened to me here."

At least she had gotten that out—simple, honest, and straightforward. Speaking the words aloud had made them feel even more real, even though she had known she had them for a long time now.

She looked up at him, scanning his face for any sign that he might not feel the same way. She had passed the ball to him and she could only hope he didn't throw it right back at her. After a few moments, a slow, warm smile spread over his face.

"That'll be quite a long time, then. My plans have changed. Instead of leaving to start a new restaurant, I'm partnering up with my current head chef who'll manage the opening in Boston. I'll be here to stay. I *want* to stay." He pressed his knee against hers. "I want to spend more time with you, too. I've been developing feelings for you ever since our first pottery class."

"Really?" Grace's face lit up, her heart seeming to expand in her chest.

"Definitely. You've made me realize that there's more to life than just working myself sick." He took her hand and squeezed it. "I haven't taken a moment to stop and look at all the things I've done or all the friends I've made. But I should. Like you said, there's a lot out there to explore, and I want to explore it with you."

His expression turned shy, and Grace could have sworn he was blushing. It endeared him to her more than ever.

"What's up?" she asked, chuckling.

"It's just been a really long time. But in some ways, it's like I was waiting for you. I couldn't have guessed that all the things I wanted could be in one person."

Grace thought back to their golf date, when she had thought the same thing. "I couldn't have guessed that either, but here we both are."

He beamed and kissed her, the sweetness leftover from the ice cream on his lips. Grace's whole body warmed despite the chilly cup in her hands, her excitement almost feeling electric. She finally felt like she knew what she wanted—like she was finally following her heart again.

* * *

Joshua gave Grace one last light peck before pulling back, looking into her hazel eyes. Everything about her was beautiful, inside and out, and being with her made him feel more alive and hopeful than he had felt in a long, long time. Every word he'd said was true, coming straight from a spot inside him that he'd thought he closed off for good. Telling her how he felt made a weight that he didn't know he was carrying disappear.

They both smiled, leaning into each other. Joshua felt like he was jumping off a cliff, but in a good way, as if there was a safe, deep ocean underneath him. He was used to taking risks and going for what he wanted in his business. It had become second nature at this point. Now he was finally doing it for himself.

These feelings between him and Grace were real, and he just knew it was going to be special.

It already was.

"Want to keep walking?" he asked. "I'm a little too energetic after all that to sit still."

Grace laughed. "Yeah, let's."

He helped her to her feet, tossing both of their empty cups into the garbage, and held onto her hand. She linked their fingers together as if they'd held hands just like this for years. They walked down the boardwalk, high on the bliss of their new relationship. Since they had all the time in the world now, they meandered slowly, enjoying each other's company without saying much at all.

"Let's swing by Ariana," Joshua said after a while. "There should be an open spot for us."

Grace agreed, and they turned off the boardwalk, heading toward Ariana. It was between the lunch and dinner rush, so the place wasn't as packed as it often got during peak times. Joshua nodded hello to the host and guided Grace back to a small booth in the corner that gave them a little privacy.

"Sit tight," he told her. "I'll bring something out."

"Another surprise?" Grace asked, her eyes bright with excitement.

"Of course." He grinned and headed back into the kitchen, where the chefs were prepping meals for the night's service.

"You're here?" Connor asked, looking up at him in confusion. "I thought you were out and about."

"I was. I am, kind of. I'm not on the clock, I'm just here looking for some good wine." Joshua disappeared into the wine cellar, taking his time to find just the right bottle of wine. One that screamed Grace.

He ran his hands along the bottles until he found a refreshing, slightly dry white wine that they had just gotten in. It would be perfect, especially for the small treat he was going to whip up. He found an empty prep spot and threw together some of the crostinis that she had loved when she'd come into the restaurant with Angela and Lydia.

He grabbed two glasses on his way out, balancing the plate on his arm, and went back to the table. Grace's face lit up again when she saw him.

"It's not much, but I figured this occasion was worth a little treat." He put down the crostini and poured them each a glass of wine.

"Not much? This is amazing," Grace said, accepting her glass of wine. "To the future."

"To the future." Joshua lightly tapped his glass against hers and took a sip. He couldn't wait to see what more was in store for them.

CHAPTER TWENTY-FOUR

"Oof, what's in here?" Angela asked, putting down one of Grace's boxes in her new apartment. It was labeled 'living room,' but Angela had no idea what would be so heavy. "Weights?"

"Actually, they might be. I had a few hand weights," Grace called from inside her master bedroom. "Sorry!"

"Don't be sorry. I needed to hit the gym anyway." Angela laughed and opened the box. "Yup, it's weights!"

Angela started to unpack them, putting the weights next to Grace's yoga mat. Lydia had turned on some upbeat pop music to help them pass the time as they helped their friend get settled into her new place. Angela had to dance a little as she crossed the room again to grab another box from near the door. There were only a few more boxes left on the dolly they'd borrowed from Grant.

She picked up a lighter box this time, looking around the apartment to find a path to the kitchen without tripping over empty boxes. Jennifer had done a great job helping Grace find the apartment. It was beautiful, and it would look incredible once Grace had a chance to decorate more and put her little personal touches around the place.

"Mommy, look!" Jake called from a corner. He popped out of an empty box, a big grin on his face. "It's a little fort!"

"It is!" Angela laughed, thankful he had finally found a way to stay out of everyone's path. He wanted to help, but his version of "helping" mostly consisted of playing with tape and doodling on boxes.

Angela put down the box and opened it up. There were just a few things like kitchenware inside, so she took it to the kitchen.

"We only have two boxes left to move from next to the door," Angela told Grace, who was unpacking some dishes.

"Really? Wow." Grace leaned against the counter. "I guess that means I'll have a lot more stuff to buy, huh? Furniture, sheets, a desk... I guess I shipped less stuff from Colorado than I thought."

"But decorating is the fun part!" Angela grinned.

"Of course it is to you!" Grace snorted. "I'm so excited that you're going to help me decorate. I'm really grateful."

Angela was looking forward to flexing her interior design skills. They had already sat down to figure out the general vibe Grace wanted to go for. It was going to be simple and fresh, the kind of place that was a perfect solace after a long day.

"No problem at all! I'd feel like a bad friend if I didn't offer to help." She looked out the kitchen window, which had an incredible view of the water. "And this place is stunning—so light and airy. It's already very 'you,' but it's going to be perfect once we get started."

"I know you'll make it look gorgeous." Grace's phone buzzed on the counter and she looked down at it, her face lighting up. "Oh, good!"

"What's up?"

"I got a message back from a couple who wanted some photos taken. They'd like to book me!" Grace rapidly typed on her phone. "They were at Patrick's book signing. Kelsey was the wife's name."

"Oh, right! That's great!" Angela knew Kelsey in

passing since she worked at the antique store that Angela loved to frequent.

"It is. It looks like I've been doing a lot of accidental networking since I got here." She typed for a few more moments before hitting send. "I've made so many great connections."

"What just happened?" Lydia asked, coming out of Grace's bedroom. There was a piece of clear plastic tape stuck to her t-shirt, which Angela pulled off.

"I booked a family photo shoot with some people I met at Patrick's book signing!" Grace told her.

"Congrats! That's so amazing. Looks like you'll be busy." Lydia grinned.

Angela had to grin too. There was no hiding how excited they both were that Grace was sticking around. She had slid right back into their friendship like no time had passed, just as Angela and Lydia had done when they'd reconnected.

Now Angela couldn't imagine the island without Grace there. Rachel probably wasn't going to move her entire family from Chicago to the island, but now that all of them were here, she was sure to come back and visit more. She'd even floated the idea of bringing her daughter, who was around Jake's age, to continue the tradition of summer friendships.

"So, so busy," Grace said, pushing some stray hair that had fallen out of her ponytail back into place. "And I'm doing a collection for Nicole's gallery on top of that. I've missed doing my creative work too, so it should be a nice change of pace. Plus, I have these views as inspiration."

"These views are truly amazing," Angela said.

There was a heavy *thump* in the living room, and all three women looked at each other. Angela rushed out to find Jake halfway inside a box, which had tipped over. He giggled and crawled out of it, not even noticing the worried look on Angela's face. She sighed with a smile, shaking her head.

"You're okay?" Angela asked Jake.

"Mm-hm." Jake popped to his feet. "The castle tipped over, though."

"So it's a castle now?" Lydia asked, leaning against the wall.

"Yup!"

"It sounds like a lot of fun." Grace leaned onto the counter so she could see Jake through the opening. "Want to help open up those last two boxes?"

Jake nodded and headed over to the last two boxes. Angela helped him peel off the tape, revealing some beautiful throw pillows and a metal sculpture of a lion. Jake put the lion sculpture on the windowsill, and Angela took the pillows into Grace's bedroom. Grace and Lydia did the last box, which held some supplies for Grace's eventual desk.

"All done! I think this requires a toast," Grace said. "How about lemonade?"

"Yes, please! That sounds so refreshing right now," Angela said. "I'm so thirsty."

Grace went into the fridge, which was stocked with some basic groceries, and found the glasses she had unpacked. She filled each one with lemonade and passed them around.

"To the future," she declared, raising her glass.

"To the future," everyone echoed, tapping their glasses against each other.

* * *

Grace had finally settled into her apartment enough to know where everything was. After a week of opening and closing five drawers just to find her wine opener or digging through her closet to find that one top she wanted to wear, she was happy to finally have a morning where she could go about things on autopilot and be out the door on time.

She headed down to the docks, camera bag in

tow, looking along the rows of boats until she found the one she was looking for. Joshua was sitting on the deck, looking out onto the water. She couldn't help but smile. His boat suited him—it wasn't too flashy or too big. He had bought it because he'd always wanted one, but he'd told her once that he hadn't taken it out nearly enough. Today, though, it would be put to good use.

"Hey, welcome aboard," Joshua said, helping Grace onto the small boat. Once she was securely on the deck, he kissed her gently on the lips.

"Wow, this is great." Grace swiveled her head back and forth, looking around a little.. "I'm so excited to give it a spin."

"Hopefully it'll be the first of many little trips." He smiled, adjusting his baseball hat, and started up the boat to pilot them out of the dock.

Grace couldn't wait. He had promised her that he'd take her out often since the views were even better than the one outside of her apartment. The sounds of the docks slowly faded as they pulled out of the harbor and into the open water. Grace pulled out her camera and started taking a few test shots. She grinned, looking at the snapshots in the viewfinder. She had high expectations of the views that morning, and they had already been exceeded.

"Even the test photos are gorgeous. I can't wait until we pass by Nantucket and Martha's Vineyard," she said excitedly.

"And we should visit them sometime too. It's a nice trip by boat," Joshua commented, slowing the vessel down a little bit.

Grace turned back toward the island and took a few snapshots before walking over to Joshua to show him.

"That looks great," he said with a warm smile. "I sometimes forget that Marigold isn't very big until I see it from a distance. Or we're farther out than I thought we were."

"Yeah, same." She rested her camera on her lap and sat down next to Joshua. "It's kind of like Mary Poppins and her bag. It holds a lot, but it doesn't look very big. It's a miracle that I found a place as perfect as I did. "

"It is. How's the new apartment treating you? Are you settled in?" he asked.

"Yup, finally! I know where everything is now." Grace laughed. "And I've gotten my routes to the store and to the inn down pat. It's so easy to get from place to place."

"Those first days at a new place are always the most annoying. It's like you unpacked and put everything in its own spot just a few days ago, but you can't remember where stuff is."

"It's maddening!"

The boat lazily drifted past another teeny island that looked mostly uninhabited, at least from where they were. Grace took a few shots of that too.

"How are things at the restaurant?" she asked, adjusting her dark ponytail as it got tousled in the breeze.

"Great." Joshua's smiles still made butterflies flutter in her stomach. "It's been a big shift, but mostly in my head. Connor's doing great as head chef, and Alan is starting his move to Boston to open the other restaurant."

"Things are moving fast with the new restaurant."

"They are. Alan is eager, and I'm more than happy to let him take the reins. It's been nice being present at Ariana again. I'm not thinking about every next step I have to take or whatever meetings I need to be in for the new restaurant," he said with a shrug, adjusting his hat again as the wind got under the bill. "But at the same time, I don't feel like I have to be there every minute of every day. I hired good people, so I should just let them do their thing."

"That's wonderful."

"It is. Especially since I get to spend time with you," he murmured, taking her hand and giving it a squeeze. His smile softened, but it didn't become any less warm.

The butterflies in Grace's stomach flapped around even harder. How was she so at ease with him, while at the same time he made her feel like this? Not that she minded—it was the perfect combination. She felt safe with him, but he could make her feel just as giddy as she did when she was younger and had a crush. Of course, this was better in every way. She knew what she wanted in life and in a partner, and Joshua had it all.

She got up again, taking in the scenery again before turning to take a quick photo of Joshua when he wasn't looking. He gave her a wink when he realized what she had done.

They drifted past another few islands until they reached the open ocean.

"Let's stop here," Grace said after another few moments, going off of a gut feeling rather than any geographical marker.

Joshua killed the power to the boat as Grace pulled out the bag filled with her father's ashes. He sat with her on the boat's edge, the wind at their backs, and looked at her without saying a word.

Grace nodded and opened the bag, beginning to sprinkle the ashes into the ocean.

Joshua sat close to her as she spread the ashes, the wind catching some and sending them off into the deep blue water. They both watched as the last of the ashes drifted away. Joshua slipped an arm around Grace and she leaned into him, her body against his, soothed by the steady rhythm of his heartbeat.

"Goodbye, Dad," Grace whispered. "I love you."

Something unwound itself in her chest, something that she had lost sight of in the time since her father's passing even though it was always a little bit present. The grief was still there, and part of her knew that sadness would never go away entirely, but she had known her father's death was coming for a long time. She had grieved for him for a long time too.

But she knew that above all, he had always wanted her to be happy. And she was finding that happiness more and more every day.

She took a gentle breath, smelling the salt of the ocean and Joshua's warm, spicy cologne. It all smelled like home to her now.

"I'm ready to keep going," Grace said, giving Joshua's hand a little squeeze.

"All right." He gently kissed the top of her forehead and went back to the captain's seat. "Let's go."

Grace smiled at him as he started the boat again. She was ending one chapter of life and starting another, with Joshua and all of her friends, new and old, at her side.

* * *

The series continues in Beachside Weddings. Wedding bells, natural disasters, and new neighbors make for a busy fall on Marigold Island. Catch up with Lydia, Angela, and all of their family and friends!

Click HERE to get your copy and continue your journey with the characters on Marigold Island.

ABOUT THE AUTHOR

Fiona writes sweet, feel-good contemporary women's fiction and family sagas with a bit of romance.

She hopes her characters will start to feel like old friends as you follow them on their journeys of love, family, friendship, and new beginnings. Her heartwarming storylines and charming small-town beach settings are a particular favorite of readers.

When she's not writing, she loves eating good meals with friends, trying out new recipes, and finding the perfect glass of wine to pair them with. She lives on the East Coast with her husband and their two trouble-making dogs.

Follow her on her website, Facebook, or Bookbub.

Sign up to receive her newsletter, where you'll get free books, exclusive bonus content, and info on her new releases and sales!

ALSO BY FIONA BAKER

The Marigold Island Series

The Beachside Inn

Beachside Beginnings

Beachside Promises

Beachside Secrets

Beachside Memories

Beachside Weddings

Made in the USA
Monee, IL
11 September 2025